One Paddle
of a Lock

Mike Simmons

Cover design and illustrations by Alan Padwick
Proof reading and Editing Fran Thorne

ISBN
9798713069476

British Library Cataloguing in Publication Data
A catalogue record for this book is available from the British Library

To my editor and proof reader

Fran Thorne

&

My good friend Adel McMahon
who is credited with the title

Contents

CHAPTER ONE

The Three Wise Men

The red-faced, flustered skipper swore in frustration as his sixty-foot-long narrowboat drifted uncontrollably towards a line of moored boats. A strong breeze blew across the wide expanse of the marina, making safe passage to the fuel point on the opposite side distinctly unpredictable. Throttle on, throttle off, engine roaring. The tiller bar pushed first one way then the other, but still the unresponsive bow end flipped and flopped in defiance of any attempted control.

His wife, standing at the sharp end and displaying mild panic, had armed herself with the long wooden boat pole. He waved to her and shouted, but any attempt at instruction was lost to the sound of the thumping machinery underneath his feet.

Crockenhill Marina had until recently been unmolested arable farmland. Selling it to the company wanting to build a marina had no doubt proved lucrative for both landowner and the marina shareholders, who were very aware of the shortage of mooring places on the overcrowded 140km canal and the network generally. With a national housing shortage many, particularly the young, regarded living on a boat as a cheaper option to renting, but they still had to be moored somewhere. So, for developers countrywide, the idea of digging a big hole, putting in some pontoons, a few facilities, then filling it with water seemed like a lucrative plan.

Resting between the busy main road into town on one side and the winding narrow canal on the other, the marina covered a large area, accommodating over two hundred boats. Most, though not all, were wide beams or narrowboats. These were moored alongside slatted wooden finger pontoons which, when wet or peppered in geese droppings, were, to say the least, challenging. For those individuals unfortunate enough to fall in, either by accident or inebriation, metal ladders were provided at certain places to aid their rescue, along with the obligatory life rings.

To reach the entrance of the marina from the main road you had to navigate a long track, with the emphasis on the word 'track' which was riven with deep potholes, testing the most robust of cars' suspension. When it rained a clay type mud splattered anything that moved, whilst in dry weather a thin layer of dust blew into and onto every crevice and surface imaginable.

At the far side of the marina, next to the pump out and fuel filling point, stood a ranch-like wooden building with a veranda, though no rocking chair or spittoons. It would not have been out of place on an American spaghetti western film set. Inside various services were provided; an office, social space and a shop that sold an assortment of groceries. A small library of second-hand books and DVD's was available to those bored with television, Brexit or life in general. Toilets and showers were available for anyone preferring more space to perform their daily ablutions. It was though, a debatable point why boaters became reliant on external facilities, worse still appeared quite aggrieved if they were unavailable for use.

To the newcomer, those visiting, and boaters already moored in the marina, it had a welcoming and comfortable ambience where no end of people were willing to help or offer advice, even if it wasn't sought or required.

It was outside the ranch building, on that gusty day, that the three wise men, Bruce, Bert and Jeb, themselves victims of the notorious crosswinds, watched as the steerer was blown ever nearer to a line of moored boats, whilst his poor wife became ever more hysterical.

This trio of senior citizens drank tea from large mugs and muttered amongst themselves. Had this action been happening on their side of the marina they would without doubt have offered some assistance. But marinas have an unspoken social order and cliques are rife. This, as in most close communities is fuelled often by gossip, (the twitching curtain syndrome) and a mild infusion of one-up-manship, albeit on a subconscious level.

As one long term moorer, Mavis Brown, was heard to say to her neighbours, 'Oh we have bow thrusters and a reverse layout.' The young couple had neither. In fact, Mavis harboured a secret irritation with the newly arrived couple as their boat was not aesthetically acceptable to be moored next to hers, being a bit rusty with peeling paint. They also had a cat and she hated cats.

Mavis Brown would have been much happier had they and their carnivorous mammal been dispatched to the Dark Side of the marina, where another social order reigned, but that is for another chapter.

Bruce was in his mid-sixties and had recently retired from a lifetime of working. He and his wife Julia had owned their wide beam, Carpet Bagger, for some years but only ever had the time to jolly off at weekends and holidays. Now they could spend their retirement cruising the canals. At least that was the intention.

'He's got himself right across the front of all those boats now,' Bruce said, draining the last of his tea from the mug.

Bert took a drag on his thin roll-up and grumbled. 'He should have given it more wellie. They never give it enough wellie.'

Jeb said, 'It's alright for you to say, he might be new to boating, we all had to learn once.' 'Well I'm glad it's not my boat he's bashing into,' replied Bert.

Bruce laughed. 'Miserable old goat, you've never been the same since you had that new knee.'

Bert and his wife Muriel, or Mur as he called her, had moved onto their narrowboat after retiring, he as a plumber and she as a checkout supervisor at a large food retailer.

Mur had been in to see Linda, the marina manager, to complain about poo deposited near her jetty. Unsure of the origin or species of said object a picture had been taken on her smartphone as evidence, this she eagerly showed to anyone who showed an interest, though she did resist sharing it on social media. Putting down her cheese sandwich Linda grimaced at this image of canine excrement.

'It's difficult to do anything without knowing who's dog it is,' she said.

Muriel though, had a suggestion. 'DNA', she retorted loudly, 'there should be DNA samples of all the dogs on the marina, then the poo could be tested and matched.'

Linda's eyes rolled and she smiled politely. 'Well, I suppose it's an idea,' she said.

'I'll send you the picture,' Mur called on reaching the door. 'Maybe you could circulate it on email.' Linda threw the remainder of her lunch in the bin.

Bert and Muriel would not have been out of place at a caravan club rally, steam fair or in the Ancient Order of Buffalos. They 'belonged' and guarded their 'membership' of this 'club' jealously. Had there been a social committee he would have been chairman and she secretary. Membership would be at their favour and all social arrangements bear their stamp of approval. This though only existed in the Ranch sector of the marina where the building acted as a meeting point for its occupants. The other three sectors had their own social order and characters.

Jeb lived alone. He always had and preferred it that way. He was though a sociable character and much liked, recognisable in his shorts or holed grey tracksuit bottoms.

He enjoyed chewing the cud with other boaters, with a bottle of Shiraz at his elbow and his smelly pipe clasped in his mouth, though the seclusion of his seventy foot narrowboat, Grey Pearl, always beckoned, where he could read and paint whilst listing to his beloved Mozart. In the five years that he had been at the marina people knew very little about him, other than he had mentioned that he used to live in the South West. There was some family, but they rarely visited, not that it seemed to worry him.

The gusty wind had dropped slightly, though this was too late for the skipper whose craft was now sideways across the bows of other moored narrowboats, as if held by a magnetic force. Anybody on board their boat would have felt the hard bump as it collided into them. Some emerged to complain and check their paintwork, whilst others were happy to assist. Unfortunately, the more verbal advice the skipper received from the other boaters, the more flustered he became; he was clearly very embarrassed at his dilemma.

A tall young guy in his early thirties jumped from the bow of his own boat onto the stern of the languishing vessel.

'Hi guys. I'm Jimmy,' he said, the breeze blowing his long blonde hair across his bronzed complexion.

'Shall we see if we can get this boat off?'

The exasperated skipper readily agreed. 'It would be great if you could, I've made a bit of a pig's ear.'

His wife, who was clearly younger than him, was still standing at the bow end, boat pole in hand. She thought it was like being rescued by a young Viking and watched intently as his suntanned limbs prepared to battle the elements.

Jimmy had river water coursing through his veins. Until retiring last year his father had skippered a tug for Cory's on the River Thames, towing the huge barges of rubbish from Wandsworth to Gravesend. His grandfather and great grandfather had both been tug skippers in the old London Docks, and his two uncles currently operated pleasure craft from Waterloo Pier.

After leaving school Jimmy got an apprenticeship with The Port of London Authority. Two years later, with the help of his dad, he bought his first narrowboat, a thirty foot 'tub' called Swift, although it was anything but. The PLA allowed him to moor in Lime House Basin, near Canary Wharf, whilst he was working on the river. This is where he had met his partner Eva. She worked behind the bar at the Grapes, a pub he often frequented until late into the evening, which also sold the best fish and chips around

Eventually Jimmy and Eva pooled their resources, sold Swift, and bought a sixty-foot narrowboat with a cruiser stern, which they named Rainbow, after the Greenpeace ship Rainbow

Warrior. Their contented lives were to be altered forever though, when a year later Jimmy, along with others was made redundant. He was devastated, working on the river was all that had ever known. Faced with having to move the boat from Lime House dock they decided to leave London and start a new life in another part of the country. But where? The answer came when Jimmy saw an advertisement for an Assistant Harbour master at Bristol docks. Being amply qualified he applied, was successful, and their journey west began.

They were both proud Eco Warriors having been members of Greenpeace and Friends of the Earth before Extinction Rebellion or Greta Thunberg had ever been thought of. Jimmy and Eva believed with a passion that people should, where possible, be self-sufficient and not over reliant on a global support system that could fail at any time. Like Lewis and Jodie, their neighbours, in Crockenhill Marina they had acquired a nearby allotment. Not that they had known anything about growing vegetables, but they were willing students of the more seasoned gardeners who, like them, were pleased with their first year's crop.

Jimmy pushed the tiller bar hard over to starboard and eased the throttle forward. He pressed the stem hard into the bow fender of a moored boat and increased the revs. Slowly the stern end started moving away from the line of boats. When it had shifted sufficiently, he straightened the tiller bar and eased the throttle into reverse before applying maximum revs. Taking the power off he allowed the boat to glide backwards then, with enough open water between him and the moored boats, he leant hard on the tiller and pushed the throttle down. The sixty foot 'boat swung in the direction of the fuel point and minutes later Jimmy brought it alongside.

The skipper who had introduced himself as Lawrie couldn't thank Jimmy enough. His poor wife was just glad to be on land again.

'That was great, Jimmy, bloody great! You've clearly done this before.'

Jimmy laughed. 'Yeah, a few times.'

'See,' said Bert, turning to Bruce and Jeb. 'Gave it plenty of wellie, that's what you 'ave to do.'

Jeb laughed. 'I didn't see you offering to help.'

Bert shrugged, ground his fag end into the gravel and walked off with Muriel in the direction of their boat.

Lawrie's wife, Toni, had recovered from her ordeal and was glad to be on firm ground once again. She stepped from the boat onto the jetty holding a bottle of chilled white wine.

'Just a little something, for helping us out,' she said, gazing up into Jimmy's bright blue eyes.

'No prob guys, but you don't need......'

'Oh please,' she said, 'take it.' Take me as well, she thought, a lusting shiver running through her slim, frustrated body.

Lawrie interrupted. 'Thanks Jimmy,' he laughed. 'We might have been stuck there all night. Now we better get some fuel before it closes.'

Toni watched as her rugged Viking rescuer walked off, his plump buttocks tight inside his cut down jeans.

'Nice lad,' said Lawrie. 'Shall we empty the loo while we're here?'

She half closed her eyes, took a deep breath and sighed. God, she wished he wouldn't wear bloody socks with those sandals. Still at least the knee length khaki shorts had gone.

'Alright dear,' she sighed, taking one last look down the road at the Viking rescuer.

CHAPTER TWO

Theft

There is nothing more tranquil than watching a family of swans emerge from the morning mist and glide serenely and peacefully across still waters. This however was an illusion. The male who headed up this bevy, let's call him Ronnie, was a psychopathic thug who would stop at nothing to defend his territory and family.

In the middle of the marina was a small island, not yet inhabited, although colonisation had been suggested by boaters seeking to withdraw further from society's-imposed conventions. Independence had been muted, and even a flag. It was here on this grassy mound that the swans, undisturbed by human footprint, used to nest and hatch their eggs. Then, for reasons known only to the breeding habits of a mute swan, they decided to build a nest at the end of a jetty on the Canal Side sector of the marina.

The inhabitants of this sector were in the main a peaceful Nordic lot who bore no malice to man or beast. Not as visual or vocal as moorers in the Ranch Sector, they preferred instead the communal seclusion of their own space and, to a man or woman, would have been appreciative and protective of the marina's wildlife. This concept though would soon wear thin, as Ronnie's aggression increased.

Lewis shouted, 'Shit! That bloody thing!' He was bending down holding his leg.

His partner Jodie, hearing the commotion, dropped the duvet she was changing and went into the saloon.

'Whatever's the matter?' she asked.

'That bloody swan just attacked me,' he said, lifting his leg. 'Look.'

Jodie could see a long red mark just below his kneecap.

'Well, what were you doing?' she asked.

'Doing?' he shouted angrily. 'All I was doing was walking down the jetty. They're nesting right on the edge. Vernon needs to do something about it'.

Jodie laughed. 'Like what? You were feeding them this morning.'

'Well, I won't be anymore,' he grumbled. 'Let them starve.'

She chuckled then went back to changing the duvet.

Ronnie's reign of terror lasted three months. People attempting to use the jetty were hissed at, spat at and generally intimidated. All other feathered residents or visitors were either driven away or banished to another part of the marina. This only ceased when the cygnets had grown to a size where Ronnie considered them safe from predators. Ronnie was clearly oblivious to Lewis and Jimmy planning a meal of roasted swan. 'A great favourite with Henry V111 apparently,' they had said.

Jodie laughed when Lewis had mentioned it. 'And I suppose you and Jimmy are going to catch and cook it.'

'Easy,' he said, 'just creep up behind it, then bop.'
She shook her head. 'Yeah right, this is a man who couldn't even kill an eel last week.'

'Well, that was different,' he retorted. 'It was slippery and writhing about.'

'You're pathetic,' she said, throwing a cushion at him.

Lewis and Jodie were moored next to Jimmy and Eva. Being of a similar age the lads shared an illegal recreational interest, which along with several cans of lager they would smoke well into the night. The girls preferred a bottle of Prosecco and catching up with Love Island and the soaps on television. Neither Jimmy nor Lewis could understand how two intelligent women could 'watch such crap,' as they put it.

There is almost zero crime reported in the marina, although it is becoming much more common on the canals; the occasional pair of panties stolen from the communal washing machine or rusting bike from the stand, but nothing to ripple the normally calm waters. There was a suspicion as to the identity of the pantie thief, but until he was caught wearing or sniffing them there was little that could be done.

It was therefore concerning when, much to her bewilderment and annoyance, Jodie's jar containing over one hundred pounds of saved coins went missing from a shelf on the boat.

She didn't want to believe that this could happen here of all places. One of the reasons for moving away from London, though not the main one, was the increase in crime and anti-social behaviour. They had been fortunate not to have been victims themselves, but several of their friends had been broken into and their homes ransacked.

Lewis threw himself down onto the sofa. 'Well, don't look at me. I haven't touched it.' Although he knew she had grounds for thinking that.

'I'm not saying you did,' she retorted loudly, 'but it's gone, look.' She pointed to the gap on the shelf where the tall glass Kilner jar had once stood.

'It must have happened when we were at the allotment. I can't believe it. Someone has taken it.' She felt the tears welling in her eyes.

'Oh shit! Shit!' Lewis suddenly jumped up from the sofa and grabbed a round tin marked Tea. Quickly removing the lid, he breathed a sigh of relief.

Jodie steamed. 'That's all you're worried about, that bloody weed.'

Vernon, Linda's partner and the co-manager of the marina, was not happy.

'Someone's shit all over the floor in the men's toilet,' he shouted, storming into the ranch building, his already florid complexion turning an angry puce colour. There was little point in attempting a distraction, Vernon was too consumed with the purveyor of human waste that he would have to clean up. Lewis and Jodie waited instead until Linda had finished her phone conversation in the office, not that she had heard much of it, with Vernon ranting louder than normal in the background.

Linda made some coffee and sat down on the sofa with the aggrieved pair. She posed all the questions that an amateur sleuth would ask before agreeing that the police should be called in.

The police came the next day. They called at the office first where, after drinking cups of coffee, Linda directed them to Lewis and Jodie's boat in the Canal Side sector. There were two of them. One was very young. Jodie wondered if he was old enough to drive.

The other, an older and more experienced cop, wore a black polo shirt underneath his stab vest. Body art covered his thick arms and a pair of black wraparound sunglasses rested on the top of his mousey brown cropped hair. Lewis wasn't very old, but he still remembered when policemen looked like policemen, not Rambo impersonators. Jodie and the older officer sat down in the saloon. The younger one lingered casually next to Lewis by the door. He seemed more interested in what it was like living on a boat than the robbery.

'Must be a cheap way of living?' he asked. Lewis shook his head. 'Not always mate.'

'Me and my girlfriend are renting now, bloody expensive, we're trying to get a deposit together,' he added.

'That's great,' said Lewis, 'good luck with that.' He hoped that was the end of the questions. Officer 'Rambo' now comfortably settled on the sofa, took a notebook from his pocket.

'You said the boat wasn't locked when you went out?' he asked Jodie.

'Well, people don't,' she said defensively. 'It's the way it is in here, people trust each other.' He chuckled. 'Don't tell the insurance company that.'

Lewis added. 'I'm sure it wouldn't be anybody in the marina, we know most of them.'

The officer turned the volume down on his chattering radio. 'What about somebody coming in from outside the marina, is that possible?'

'Unlikely,' said Jodie. 'Any stranger would be noticed and challenged.'

'By whom?' asked the younger one, now sitting on the steps leading to the front door.

'Well, anyone,' said Jodie, slightly flustered.

'That's right,' added Lewis quickly. 'People look out for each other in here'.

Rambo nodded, wrote something down in his notebook, then chewed the end of his biro.

'Cameras?' he asked, abruptly.

Lewis shook his head. 'There aren't any over here,' he answered.

Rambo stood up and sniffed. 'Shame, we might have got something from them. Now you're sure there's nothing else missing?'

Lewis looked nervously across at the tin marked Tea. 'No nothing else.'

The notebook was closed and dropped into his pocket. 'I'll get 'SOCO' to call round tomorrow, but I think you'll have to put this one down to experience. Be a little less trusting in future and lock your doors when you leave the boat.'

'I quite fancy this life myself,' said the young cop, as they left the boat and walked off along the pontoon.

'Well! A fat lot of good they were,' said Jodie, closing the door.

Lewis poured two large glasses of white wine and handed one to Jodie.

'What did you expect? They were hardly 'Hercule Poirot.' I can't believe it could be someone in the marina though.'

Jodie sat on the sofa and took a large gulp. She needed it. 'Well, if it's not, then who?' she sighed.

'You didn't really think that I............?' he protested.

She interrupted him. 'No, of course not love, you promised.'

He sat down next her. 'I really am finished with all that hard stuff,' he said, pouring some more wine. Outside they heard an owl calling to the night.

'I know,' she said resting her head on his shoulder.

CHAPTER THREE

Seasons

A stretch of grass, tufted and coarse, sat between the jetty and the high hedge bordering the marina and the Canal Side sector. On the other side of the hedge was another track and a long line of boats moored at the side of the canal. At the far end near the high security gate stood an ancient green crane called Neal, which was purely decorative and serving no practical purpose. Alongside this were two rows of wooden sheds. Weathered and dull, their exteriors mirrored unloved beach chalets in an out of season seaside town. Jimmy and Eva could never understand why anyone living on a boat would need a shed. 'Surly the idea is not to hoard stuff,' she had insisted on many occasions.

Eva liked to dabble in poetry and penned 'Sunny Sands' on a wet and windy day.

> *It's an out of season seaside town*
> *Here at sunny sands*
> *Where ghosts of August children*
> *Haunt the sleeping coloured trams*
> *And shuttered hotel windows*
> *Like blind men strain to see*
> *Into the face of the winter storm*
> *As it dances from the sea*

Seagulls now occupy castles in the sand
Their creators long returned to dark cities far inland.
The walls they built with eager hands
to stop the rising tide
Have, like a scar upon the skin,
Faded into time.

They both led a frugal lifestyle. Waste was kept to a minimum and they recycled as much as they could. Jimmy had fitted solar panels to the roof of the boat keeping his leisure and engine batteries charged up and providing additional power free of use.

Eva did have one addiction though; charity shops. She would spend the day with friends going from one shop to the other in search of bargains for her and Jimmy. He wasn't interested though, given the opportunity he would spend his life in a tee shirt and cut down jeans.

Access to the marina from the canal was by way of a narrow entrance. A lift bridge, not uncommon on European rivers and canals, enabled boats to pass underneath when raised and cars to pass over when dropped. This navigable passage was at the opposite end of the grassy stretch on the Canal Side sector and divided the Nordic community from the Dark Side across the water.

Whilst a village has its local pub and a town its square, the marina had wooden benches, in various states of repair, placed liberally on the grass strips around the perimeter. Here on warm summer evenings the dwellers and boaters of this aquatic community would meet to parlay and consume. The hardy amongst them even braved the cold and chilled winds of autumn and winter sitting huddled together like sheep against a hedgerow. Their often mundane and repetitive ramblings could though be tickled and titillated by the appearance of the unusual, a Waitrose food delivery van, an undertaker's private ambulance, or the Fire Service called to pump out a sinking boat. All three though were a rare occurrence.

Alan, Jock and Archie had little time for the sedentary musings of their neighbours as the twang of plectrum on strings backed by the thud of bass and snare amplified itself across the otherwise quiet and lazy Canal Side sector. The accompanying chords and vocals would roll and pitch as the symmetry of the rehearsal sometimes waned in pursuance of performance standards. Further rhythmic imbalance occurred as the pile of empty beer cans and group merriment increased.

Alan had arrived earlier on his powerful passion, a sleek black and chrome 1000cc motorbike. With his dreadlocks, decorated helmet and clad in black leather jacket he often disappeared into the countryside to wind his 'beast' through the lanes and roads. Open road cruising, not that type! and music were his liberation from the crushing norm of life, following early retirement. He too rented a chalet where the 'growling beast' rested after their latest joust of rubber on tarmac.

Jock Cullen was moored next to Alan. He shared his boat, Merlin, with a blasphemous old South American parrot called Nigel. His second wife, a needy and vain woman, had divorced him and after many months of financial wrangling he had left Glasgow with enough money to buy a boat, something he had always fancied.

She always hated the noisy bird and had twice attempted to dispose of it. On the second occasion, when trying to stage a suicide attempt, she had received severe pecking wounds to her hands and face, as well as being told repeatedly and loudly to - uck off. This was the last straw. It was her or Nigel she told Jock. The parrot being less vocal and cheaper to keep, he chose Nigel, then moved south.

He rented a small, one bedroom flat, in Camberwell, South London while searching for a boat to live on. It was the most depressing period of his life, even Nigel became withdrawn. It took many months in this hovel before he was told of Merlin sitting in the Didford marina in Uxbridge, West London. One visit to the boat and he knew it was the one for him and Nigel. The owners, a pleasant elderly couple, wanted a quick sale. The boat was over twenty years old, but in excellent condition, they had clearly loved and cherished it. Unfortunately, she had developed a dodgy hip and he had gout, so reluctantly they had decided to sell it. Over a drink in the General Elliot pub in Hillingdon the deal was done. Jock had the boat of his dreams and they could live out their days in their bungalow in Sidcup.

21

Having spent two years ditch crawling on the Grand Union Canal, sloshing about on muddy towpaths and an over reliance on his friend 'Johnnie Walker' Jock decided to move west and find a permanent mooring before the next winter set in. It was during this journey that he found 'Spliff.' Two days had passed since he had turned off the River Thames onto this scenic canal which meandered its way westward for 87 miles. Now he was tired and needed to find a place to moor for a few day's rest. As he exited the last lock of a small flight, he saw the tall chimney in the distance. A passing boater told him there were plenty of moorings by the old pumping station. There was only one other boat there, so he slid in behind it. The occupant, a young man with dreadlocks, was sitting underneath a tree listening to music.

After mooring up Jock went down below to fetch Nigel. He was not happy at being cooped up for so long, squawking expletives as Jock carried his cage outside into the daylight. The young man intrigued by the vocal bird wandered over. 'Hey man, my grandad had one of them, we used to teach it to swear'.

Jock laughed. 'He doesn't need any lessons.'

That night after a wee dram or two Jock crashed out early. When he awoke the following morning, he could hear the gentle patter of rain thinly smearing the roof of the boat. He checked his watch it was ten o'clock.

Venturing outside he was surprised to see that the young man had gone. He must have slept soundly as he hadn't heard him leave the mooring.

It was as he was about to step back into the boat that he heard what sounded like a cat's meow. He scanned the towpath and bank but could see no sign of a moggie, then as he opened the double stern doors fully, he saw it. On the deck, beside an empty fuel can was a small cardboard box with writing in felt pen on the side. Stacked next to it were six tins of cat meat. He opened the flaps. Inside was a small ginger coloured kitten. By the look of the scratch marks inside it had tried in vain to extricate itself from its confinement.

He carefully lifted it out, then read the writing on the box.

Hey dude. Sorry about this. Found it last week near a lock, obviously lost. You look like an animal lover and can give it a better home than I can. May see you again someday. Oli.
Oh, nearly forgot, I called it 'Spliff.

Jock smiled. 'Very apt.'

Inside the boat he sat down and lifted the little kitten onto his lap. 'So little fella, what are we going to do with you?' he said, stroking its thin body. Nigel was strangely quiet observing the small intruder with interest. 'So, what do you think Nigel, shall we keep him?' The parrot tilted its head to one side, screeched then nodded in agreement.

'Well young Spliff, it looks like you have a new home,' said Jock laughing.

The last of the autumn leaves were falling when he arrived at Crockenhill Marina on a wet and windy day. He had for once abandoned his kilt for a warmer pair of jeans. The cold breeze up his nether regions was too much to bear even for him. Once settled into the Canal Side sector he soon found kindred spirits in the 'Divorced or Separated Club' which he was amply qualified to join. Despite now living well south of the border he was still a Scotsman and was determined to wear his kilt and sporran when possible, although he tired of the comments about his underwear or sometimes lack of it. Spliff settled in well to his new surroundings making friends with Allison's aged cat, although a couple of times he had to be fished from the water. Nigel was a happy parrot as he had more people to swear at as they walked past the boat.

Outside the ranch building and near the other redundant crane, whose gib always pointed northwards, were tables and benches. Unlike the wooden version scattered around the marina, their surface was made of concrete. Jeb eased his frame onto the cold bench, flicked open his Zippo lighter and held the orange flame to the blackened rim of his Peterson pipe. There was a gurgling sucking sound as he drew the nicotine laced spittle from the bowl into the stem. He exhaled a cloud of grey smoke and sighed in satisfaction. Bert, sitting hunched on the opposite bench, was in full grumbling mode.

'That bloody thing will kill you,' he said, lighting his own fag.

Jeb coughed and shifted his buttocks from side to side. 'Don't do much for yer piles, these seats,' he chuckled.

Bert shook his head. 'Bloody ridiculous,' he said acidly. Probably got 'em for nothing, knowing this place.'

Archie had a parcel to collect from the office. He nodded to Bert and Jeb, 'Morning.'

Jeb took the pipe from his mouth. 'Heard your music last night,' he said.

'It's coming on slowly,' Archie replied, before disappearing inside.

Bert grunted. 'How can you call that bloody din music?'

Jeb raised his eyes. 'It's being 'appy that keeps you going mate.'

Minutes later Archie came out of the ranch building carrying the large parcel wrapped in brown paper.

'Not another rubber doll is it?' shouted Bert.

'How did you guess?' replied Archie, humouring him. 'I'll let you have the old one. You'll have to repair the puncture though.'

Jeb chuckled through a grey smoky haze. 'He wouldn't know what to do with it, even if he had the puff to blow it up.'

Bert shook his head and snorted. 'There's many a tune played on an old fiddle.'

Jeb laughed. 'Yeah but not one without any strings.'

Archie's sixty-foot narrowboat, Easy Rhythm, could easily have been a victim of Mavis Brown's verbal snobbery. It was several years old with the paintwork needing some attention, but it had a sound hull and it was his home. He would like to have it repainted professionally but that wasn't cheap, so would have to wait. His mooring was at the end of the pontoon on the canal side sector, close to where the swans had nested. Clearing a space on the table in front of the coal burning stove he carefully ran a sharp knife along the wide adhesive tape securing the lid of the box. Prizing open the cardboard flaps he carefully lifted out the bubble wrapped, double sided, African tribal bongos that he had found on eBay. Drumming his fingers across the taught skin he smiled with delight. 'Perfect,' he said, 'just perfect.'

The seasons dictated the volume of craft in the marina at any one time. During the summer months the wooden pontoons stood empty like gapped teeth in an open mouth awaiting food. Boaters departed the marina for an assortment of reasons. The bored and frustrated had left forever, seeking horizons new and an alternative to the narrow, overgrown and overused canal and its lack of moorings and services. This irritation was further exacerbated by an increasing number of hire boat companies and their burgeoning fleets.

It was never a good idea to engage Bert in a discussion about the growth of hire boats on the canal. His language would become distinctly fruity.

Once, when navigating a sharp bend, he was in collision with a floating stag party who were in various stages of undress and more than just a little merry. This had resulted in damage to the bow of his boat which had just been painted. Mur was equally unforgiving as she had been on the loo and had ended sprawled on the floor in a puddle of pee with knickers at half-mast.

The keen and more adventurous boaters had gone cruising for a specific period and would, some albeit reluctantly, eventually return due to work, school, or other commitments. A minority, some of whom had been afloat for many years, found their ageing body had grown weary of the lifestyle even if the mind was still willing to play. They had decided to sell up and move ashore.

Like abandoned animals, or the elderly in a care home, many of the remaining tethered craft were unloved, unkept, and rarely visited. Our three wise men often remarked that, 'people must have more money than sense, paying expensive mooring fees and never going near the boat.' Bruce thought it particularly sad, often saying, 'You can see the soul departing, just leaving a lump of floating steel behind. It's a bloody shame.'

Not all the boats in a state of disrepair and neglect were uninhabited. More commonly found hugging the banks of the canal, such a vessel would occasionally be found in a marina. Unfortunately, its occupier's lifestyle and behaviour often mirrored the exterior condition of the vessel and the norms and sensibilities, adhered to by most boaters, were abandoned.

Annie Pearce had been moored in the Ranch Sector for six months. Before that she was on the canal, licenced as a constant cruiser, not that her distance cruising was very constant, preferring instead short journeys to familiar haunts. Like Glenda, who was moored on the Dark Side, she was unique in that she communicated with 'spirit'. Not the same 'spirit' whose company the three wise men often enjoyed, although there was a similarity in the sometimes vagueness of the dialogue and communication.

She studied closely the brown coloured gunge clinging to the hull of her boat. A strong breeze seemed to be blowing the offending substance across the marina from the dark side. This was unlike any algae that she had seen before. Kneeling, she ran a stiff brush along the hull. This did little to remove its clinging mass.

Linda stood on the pontoon next to Annie watching as it accumulated and thickened on the surface. Vernon had just finished the daily ritual of raising the flags over the ranch building. On this day one of these was the Maltese National colours, a strange choice for a landlocked county in the West Country of England. Linda called him and he joined them both on the pontoon. Annie's black cat, Jingle, sat in between them showing off a recently caught mouse that was still wriggling.

Linda hesitated before offering her thoughts. 'I think It's poo,' she said. 'Someone is emptying their toilet into the marina.'

'Oh my god,' exclaimed Annie, holding her hand to her face, 'How could they? It's disgusting.'

'You know where that's coming from don't you?' offered up Vernon, pointing across the marina.

Linda nodded. 'I do.'

They had had their suspicions for some time but it was difficult to prove. Vernon offered to bring the high-pressure hose round to blast the offending gunge away from the hull. Linda said she would speak to the suspected owner tomorrow. Annie collected up Jingle and went inside her boat. Vernon kicked the now deceased mouse into the water, alongside a bald coconut that was wallowing about in the sludge.

Jodie slowly ran the tip of her finger through the film of white dust that SOCO had left on the shelf where the coin jar had stood. She picked up the framed picture of her and Lewis. It was taken when they had first moved into their rented flat in Mile End, East London. She thought fondly of the two years they had spent there, before her idyll had crashed around her. That warm September day remained seared in her memory as if it was yesterday.

The knock on the front door had been loud and urgent. Lewis had been found unconscious under a tree in Victoria Park. He had overdosed on the white stuff. They both had good jobs in the City but like many addicts there was never enough money to feed his habit. Jodie knew that he had used some of their savings to buy drugs and had threatened to leave him. There had been tears and yet more promises, he even threatened to kill himself if she left.

After many months of attending a treatment programme at the Royal London Hospital in Whitechapel, Lewis at last managed to overcome his demons. Jodie, though, had insisted that staying clean meant leaving London and its temptations, for a new life somewhere else in the country. At first Lewis had objected, citing all sorts of reasons to stay, until he realised that refusal would mean the end of their relationship.

At weekends they often left their flat in Mile End and walked alongside the Regents canal on their way to the café in Victoria park. It was a popular place for boats to moor and Lewis and Jodie had often fancied the idea of holidaying on one. So, when the wind of change finally blew, a live-aboard boat had become a real option for them.

Eva, Jimmy's partner, rapped on the side of the boat. 'Are you there, Jodie?'

'Coming,' she called, putting the picture back on the shelf.

Jodie thought how pretty Eva looked standing on the pontoon in her floral dress and long flowing red hair. Often, she thought that Eva was like a Sixties hippie and envied her carefree attitude towards life. Due to their upbringing, education, and work in London, she and Lewis had moved in a more conservative circle. But that was all behind them now, although it was taking time for them to adjust to a change of lifestyle.

'Did the fingerprint people find anything?' Eva asked.

Jodie shook her head. 'Nothing, but then I didn't think they would.'

Eva bent down to stroke Jock's cat 'Spliff', who was rubbing its body against her leg. 'I still can't believe it could be someone in the marina.'

'Maybe it wasn't,' replied Jodie.

'What do you mean?' insisted Eva, in a surprised tone.

Jodie shook her head. 'It doesn't matter. Coffee?'

CHAPTER FOUR

Boaters and Dwellers

Behind the ranch was a compound surrounded by a high wooden fence, not for the containment of horses or cattle but the storage of coal and gas bottles, and the disposal of rubbish. Banks of red paladins consumed plastic bags full of boaters' accumulated offerings. Regularly filled green bins marked, Glass only, bore testament to the boozy lifestyle of some and the occasional habits of others.

In the corner of the compound stood a small, wooden shed where self-conscious looking moorers arrived, often after dark, to undertake one of the more unpleasant aspects of living afloat, the disposal of human waste. Effluent laden cartridges, some pulled like a shopping trolley, others carried, would be lifted into the shed before being upturned and quickly poured into the round receiving bowl. Despite the use of Elson Blue, the resulting smell would rise up and sting like a swarm of bees. Following a quick rinse of the container the bearer's step from the shed taking in a deep gulp of fresh air. That should be it for another week unless relatives or friends pay a surprise visit, or sudden incontinence occurs.

For those whose boats required a regular pump out, a journey to the service pontoon was a necessity. However, unlike cartridge emptying where the pong was contained to the shed, this method of extraction created a pungent stench that assaulted the senses of anyone within inhaling distance. Our three wise men often sat and deliberated on the benches alongside the service pontoon and would have been in the firing line of this invasion of the nostrils.

The wide beam had already moored alongside when Bert, Jeb, and Bruce had sat down on the concrete topped benches. It was midday. The grey clouds which had filled the emptiness of the early morning had dissipated and warm sunshine washed over the marina. Julia, Bruce's wife had made a bread pudding which the three men were looking forward to enjoying with their morning coffee.

Jeb watched as the rotund owner of the boat bent down and connected the thick pump-out hose to the outlet hole on his gunwales. He started the machine and the connecting hose started to throb and shake as the human waste was sucked at high pressure from the tank.

'Jesus,' shouted Bert, his face contorting. 'What 'ave they been eating?'

Jeb quickly lit his cold pipe, blew out a cloud of smoke, then breathed it back in. 'That's bad,' he said, grimacing.

Bruce chuckled. 'That hose looks like it's had a dose of Viagra.' They all laughed.
Gradually the smell subsided as the tank rid itself of the last of its toxic contents.
They chuckled as the overweight owner sat exhausted on the stern of the boat, his face reddened and perspiring from the effort. His wife, a

small wispy thing, went into the office to pay the bill.

Bert laughed. 'I wouldn't mind being a fly on the wall in their bedroom, he'd probably crush 'er' Jeb went into the office to refill their coffee cups. Bruce handed round the bread pudding, which they had delayed eating until the pump out was completed.
Bert looked down on the little black spaniel sitting beside him in anticipation of a share.

'What are you after?' he said, throwing him a piece, which was rapidly consumed.

Tazz, the spaniel, belonged to Alex who was termed, the Warden, and covered for the managers, Linda and Vernon, on their two days off each week. He was, like some others in the marina, ex-military displaying a bearing and demeanour, in stark contrast to the selfish, me, me attitude portrayed by many in society.

After the wispy wife had left, Alex joined the three wise men at the table outside. Tazz ran to join him, his lead trailing in the gravel. They watched as the portly steerer edged his boat away from the service pontoon and into the middle of the marina. She waved goodbye. Alex waved back.

'Don't think he's got long for this life,' said Bert, sniffing loudly.

'She was nice,' added Alex. 'They're based at Bishops Stortford.'

'Lea and Stort, know it well,' said Bruce, standing up and stretching. 'Nice canals.'

34

Alex was moored in the Canal Side sector at the opposite end of the jetty to where Lewis and Jimmy were moored and near to the car park. His neighbour Peter, known affectionally to him as Grandad, had only recently moved his narrowboat, Kingfisher, into the Canal Side sector, having previously resided for some time in the other two. Peter often visited the Ranch Sector to socialise though preferred the more peaceful ambiance of his new mooring.

The silver Volvo drove slowly into the marina obeying the 10mph speed limit. The group watched as the driver parked in front of the ranch building. Two bored looking teenagers tumbled out of the rear of the car, handheld screens rendering any meaningful communication impossible. The parents, a middle aged, stressed looking couple, offloaded shopping, sleeping bags and holdalls. The indifferent youths reluctantly pocketed their phones to assist their parents carrying the luggage along the pontoon towards their boat.

'Sorry mate,' called Alex, as the father passed by him. 'You have to reverse the car into the car park.'

The driver looked bemused. 'Does it matter?' he asked, putting down the bags he was carrying.

'It's the rules mate. Sorry,' replied Alex. 'In case you knock someone over when pulling out.'

The driver shook his head and sighed in disbelief. 'Bloody silly rule,' he replied, walking back towards the car.

'He's not happy,' observed Bert.

Jeb chuckled. 'Nor would I be if I'd been stuck in a car with two moody teenagers for a couple of hours.'

'Weekend boaters,' said Peter.

Bert tutted. 'Probably come to wash and polish the boat again.'

'There's a lot like that,' added Jeb. 'They use the boat like a holiday cottage.'

'Well, they're not really boaters, are they?' said Peter. 'To be a boater you have to boat, get some time in, do some miles and locks.'

'He's got a point,' said Bruce. 'It's like there are two types, boaters and dwellers.'

Alex laughed. 'Don't forget the fair-weather lot, bit of rain and they moor up for the day.'

'Or don't go out in the first place,' added Bert.

'It's marinarisation,' said Jeb. 'I mean, once you come in here with all the facilities, you lose the will to go out on the cut.'

'True,' agreed Bruce. 'It gets too bloody comfortable, not that I'm complaining.'

'There's no such word as marinarisation,' said Bert.

Jeb laughed. 'Course there is. When did you last consult a dictionary?'

Peter chuckled. 'He never has, he thinks a Thesaurus is a prehistoric animal.'

'I'll 'ave you know I got a GSE in English and Woodwork at school,' retorted Bert.

'It's GCSE,' replied Jeb.

Bert shrugged. 'Well whatever it was, I got two.'

'Was that before they threw you out?' asked Bruce.

Bert contemptuously shook his head.

Earlier that year Luke had waved to the receptionists then passed through the automatic doors for the last time. He walked through the packed car park to the bus stop across the road from the entrance. The bus was full and as usual late. Before boarding he glanced over his shoulder at the Hillingdon Hospital complex which had been his place of work as a physiotherapist for the last eight years.

His partner, Ryan, finished the last of his latte in one of the busy High Street's many coffee shops. He checked his phone. The text read 'running late.' He sighed. It was only a short distance to the bus stop where he was due to meet Luke. The traffic in both directions was moving slowly and he could smell the fumes from the exhaust pipes. Several buses arrived before Luke's, disgorging their miserable looking loads onto the already crowded pavement. Luke was equally fed up after the short, cramped journey. They kissed, then walked slowly down the hill to the marina where their sixty-foot narrowboat, Otter, was moored.

The Didford marina was a small, family owned business on the 137-mile-long Grand Union Canal. In the ten years that they had owned their boat, Ryan and Luke had navigated many of its 166 locks, and beyond. In the marina they enjoyed a quiet mooring opposite a large field where cattle and horses roamed free and low early morning mists kissed the dew-soaked grass. It was a view the two men never tired of as they drew back the floral-patterned curtains that complemented the pine panelled interior. Then one day, without any warning, the bulldozers and diggers came. Now, following two years of disruptive and noisy building works, four ugly looking blocks of expensive flats had replaced this tranquil scene.

Not content with buying into this destruction, some of the residents had the gall to complain about the amount of smoke being emitted from the boats' chimneys opposite. No doubt the same ones taking their offspring the short distance to school in 4x4 cars. Luke and Ryan's decision to leave had been partly due to this development, but mainly a general weariness of daily life in an expanding and crowded London Borough. Any doubts they may have had though were eradicated following an incident one night on the way home from the cinema. Three drunken men outside one of the town's seedier establishments had seen them holding hands. As they passed, the inebriated louts subjected them to a foul tirade of abuse. This was a decisive moment in the search for pastures new.

They both knew and liked Jock, having first met him when he came to the Didford Marina to view Merlin which had been moored in front of them. The 'bonny lads', as he called them had accumulated a lot of experience and as a novice, he found their advice invaluable. After purchasing Merlin, he had decided to stay in the marina for another four weeks to acquaint himself with the boat, and of course take advantage of the club house and its cheap beer. After he had moved on, Ryan and Luke had stayed in touch by phone and skype and were pleased to hear that he had eventually secured a mooring in a place called Crockenhill Marina. With the end of summer approaching they decided to take a gentle autumn cruise, and thanks to Jock securing them a neighbouring mooring this would be the start of a new life, far away from the sprawling metropolis.

They could both remember that autumn day as the sun dipped low in the sky and they edged their narrowboat out of the bottom lock. Long shadows were starting to settle across the still waters of the canal. A chinook helicopter flew in low before disappearing over the distant tree line. Two perspiring joggers watched as Ryan pushed wearily on the balance beam to close the heavy lock gate. Clouds of midges danced franticly in the heavy air. It had been a long day and they were both exhausted.

Luke idled Otter's engine as Ryan came down the steps with the windlass and jumped onto the stern of the boat. The joggers waved as they continued their onward slog. Along the port side was a double-breasted line of green liveried hire boats, their busy season almost at an end.

Scratches and dents bore testament to their recent heavy workload, and often inexperienced skippers.

Ahead, the remains of the bridge that used to carry the railway across the canal into town, like many others though, abandoned in the Beeching cuts of the sixties. Now they could see the steel structure of the lift bridge that spanned the narrow entrance into the marina. Both men kissed. The long and eventful journey from London had been worth it

Jock and Alan were standing on the grass at the side of the entrance, both were holding a bottle of beer.

'You made it then?' called Jock.

Ryan laughed out loud. 'We nearly didn't, tell you about it later.' He was referring to catching the stern on the cill whilst descending Cowley lock on the Grand Union. Fortunately, Luke knew what to do and quickly re-flooded the chamber, resulting in no damage to the boat.

Luke took the boat out of gear. 'Where do we go?' he shouted.

Jock pointed to an empty space just along from where he and Alan were moored. Luke tweaked the throttle and pointed the bow towards the line of moored boats.

'Newcomers arriving,' said Mur, looking out of the galley window.

Bert stood up from the table, passed wind loudly then looked over her shoulder.

'It's two men, Jock and Alan seem to know them,' she said.

40

Bert sniffed. 'Probably two of their boozy friends.'

'You can talk,' she replied sharply.

Luke turned the boat sharply towards the island so that he could reverse into the mooring.

'You'll have to give it some wellie or you'll lose the nose,' shouted Bert.

'For God's sake,' said Mur, holding her ears. 'They can't hear you.'

Bert sat back down at the table, rolled a fag, then passed wind again.

Mur shook her head. 'Bloody disgusting.' She continued to watch as Luke neatly reversed the boat into the waiting mooring.

'He's done it,' she said, 'not even a bump.' Bert blew out a cloud of grey smoke. 'Not bad I 'spose,' he said, begrudgingly.

Mur shook her head, before picking up her phone and walking towards the door.

'Where you going?' asked Bert.

'To see Linda, find out who they are.'

'You nosey bitch,' called Bert, as she left the boat.

Alan took their stern line and secured it to the mooring ring attached to the pontoon.

Luke stopped the engine and they both stepped ashore.

'It's great to see you,' said Jock, smiling broadly.

'And you,' said Ryan, giving him a man hug.

'I see you're still wearing that old kilt,' said Luke.

Jock laughed. 'Can't afford anything else.'

41

'Anyone fancy a brew?' asked Alan.

'We could murder one,' replied Ryan. 'That was a lot of locks.'

CHAPTER FIVE

A Bit of Rough

The clue should have been in the daughter's name, Peachy. Vernon looked bemused as the woman bent his ear with a list of complaints that she had compiled since mooring her wide beam boat in the Ranch Sector last year. Having parked her BMW 4x4 in an awkward manner she had marched purposefully towards the ranch, a sense of entitlement oozing from every pore in her body. Peachy scurried two paces behind her mother. Chief amongst this list of woes were geese!
Vernon interrupted. 'Sorry, did you say geese?'

'Yes, geese,' she hissed loudly, emphasising the word as if he was stupid or deaf.

'And what exactly is the problem with them?' he asked, trying to stifle a smile.

'The noise,' she shrieked. 'It really is too much, especially in the morning.'
Peachy piped up. 'They woke me up the other morning, didn't they mummy?'
With her green wellies and bodywarmer Vernon thought the girl would look more at home on the arse end of a horse than on a narrowboat.

'They did,' replied the woman. 'It's quite intolerable.'

'What do you suggest we do, luv?' asked Vernon.
She bridled at being called 'luv'.

'Well, could they not be lured away or even culled?' she shouted.

Vernon forced a smile as he struggled to remain polite.

'I'll see what can be done,' he said. 'In the meantime, you could try using ear plugs.'

The woman's eyes widened and her face reddened.

'Well,' she said angrily, 'if that's your attitude, we'll have to find another marina.'

Vernon nodded. 'Maybe one without any wildlife,' he replied sarcastically.

'Come along Peachy,' she said, turning and marching out.

The girl followed, her ginger ponytail bobbing from side to side.

Bruce had been sitting on a sofa drinking strong coffee and reading a paper.

'Unbelievable,' he said. 'She's the sort that moves into a village and moans about the bloody church bells.'

Vernon sat down. 'I need a drink, a stiff one.'

Linda parked her bike against the wall of the ranch. She had cycled to the Dark Side. Someone had reported an aggressive dog which turned out to be two dogs playing, albeit roughly. How she wished people would get their facts straight before poking their noses in and complaining, but then some people had nothing better to do all day.

'Everything ok?' she asked Vernon.

Bruce laughed. 'Sore point.'

44

Vernon told her of the conversation with 'Mrs Snooty,' as he called her.

Linda shook her head. 'Unbelievable,' she replied.

Jeb sauntered in through the double doors that led to the veranda. He was wearing a wide brimmed straw hat and a pair of dark glasses.

'Alright?' asked Bruce, himself feeling more than a little delicate.

Jeb flopped down onto the sofa next to him. 'That was a heavy night,' he said, downing a pint of milk.

Bruce nodded. 'Shouldn't mix red wine and whisky; fatal.'

Vernon shouted from behind the counter. 'You two look rough,' then turned up the radio.

Jeb ignored him and closed his eyes. Bruce sipped his coffee.

'What is that crap you're listening to?' asked Bruce.

'It's Radio Two,' replied Vernon.

Jeb rolled his eyes then closed them again. 'Bloody banal rubbish.'

Bruce laughed. 'Well I suppose it's better than the Archers.'

The area in front of the Ranch showed the remnants of last night's revelry. Discarded fag ends and bottle tops were scattered on the gravel surface. Normally these would be picked up, but as the night wore on inebriation had resulted in a lack of bodily co-ordination, so the ashtrays and bins had become redundant.

Bert had left early due to a disagreement over the moon. It had been a clear night. Bruce said that the sky looked like 'a backdrop of sparkling diamonds.'

Jeb said, 'It's a full moon, amazing to think that man had walked on it once.'

Bert had replied loudly; 'It's all bloody Cobblers,' insisting that it was all filmed by the Americans in the Nevada Desert. After a heated discussion it had resulted in Bert being called 'a conspiracy theorist.' He finished his drink and stormed off back to his boat. Mur and Julia had been joined by Linda and were starting on their second bottle of red wine. They watched him flounce away. Mur laughed. 'Silly old bugger.'

It had started off as a game of *'Boules'*, or *'Bul'* as the French pronounce it. But the objective of throwing the heavy ball as close as possible to the small one was, despite the floodlights, eventually abandoned, as the players vision and balance had become more impaired. There had been talk of a barbecue, but due to the potential hygiene inadequacies of the cook, this had been cancelled for fear of an outbreak of food poisoning.

Linda retrieved an empty can of lager which had been planted in a hanging basket. Another was half buried in a tub. She was not amused at the antics, having spent much time planting and nurturing her flowers and shrubs which added a splash of colour to the otherwise dull facia of the ranch. In the corner of the *'Boules'* court lay a blue wheelbarrow, abandoned last night where the

46

giggling passenger had been tipped out onto the gravel.

Lennie was standing on the veranda looking across the marina. He was nearing thirty years old. He finished vaping, then walked through into the ranch building. 'You two look knackered,' he said, seeing Bruce and Jeb in a dishevelled heap on the sofa.

'We are,' replied Jeb, not opening his sore eyes.

Lennie laughed. 'You're getting past it, too many late nights.'

'It'll 'appen to you,' said Jeb, 'once you get a few more years under yer belt.'

'Yeah, right,' called Lennie, disappearing out of the door, and jumping on his pushbike.

Bruce stood slowly, needing another strong coffee. 'He's always in a rush.'

'Busy man,' replied Jeb. 'Not that I would want to be working on a day like this, too bloody hot.'

Julia pulled the last of her sheets from the dryer. The small room at the rear of the ranch contained three washing machines and two ineffective dryers.

'I knew that woman would be trouble,' she said.

Mavis Brown threw her smalls, or in her case not so smalls, into a washing machine. 'What woman?'

'You know, the snobby one at the end of our pontoon.'

She thought for a moment. 'Is that the one with the young girl?'

'Yes. A right little madam she is, needs a good slap.'

'So, what's she done?' asked Mavis.

Julia checked that there was nobody outside the laundry before moving close to Mavis. 'Geese,' she hissed.

'What about them?' asked Mavis.

'She and that daughter of hers were in the office earlier complaining to Vernon about the noise they make. Can you believe it. Stupid woman moves into a marina and moans about the geese.'

'What did Vernon say?' asked Mavis, putting yet another token in the box.

'He told her to get some ear plugs.'

Mavis laughed. 'Good for him. I'm surprised he didn't tell her to 'fuff' off out of the marina.'

Again, Julia checked there was nobody listening outside. 'That's not all,' she said quietly. 'Mur saw her with a young bloke the other night. They were in the car park sitting in that 4x4 of hers.'

'Well who was he?' asked Mavis.

Julia smiled. 'You'll never guess.'

Mavis shrugged. 'I don't know do I. Could be anyone.'

Relishing the moment, she drew close to Mavis's ear.

'Willie the welder!' she whispered.

Mavis's brown pebble eyes widened to gob-stopper size.

'What! Willie the welder with the greasy hair, from the boatyard?' she repeated loudly.
Julia nodded. 'Shoosh, somebody may hear you.'
Mavis was now chuckling. 'My god, who'd have thought it. Didn't his wife run off with a carpet fitter?'

'Her with all 'er airs and graces,' said Julia. 'She must like a bit of rough.'

'And what were they doing?' asked Mavis, checking the progress of her smalls.

'What do you think they were doing? The windows don't get steamed up discussing the cost of mooring fees.'

'Good grief,' smiled Mavis. 'So, she has a toy boy.'
Julia sniffed with disdain. 'He must be twenty years younger. She must be paying him! Bloody mutton.'

'You jealous?' chuckled Mavis.
Julia chortled loudly. 'You must be joking. I'd rather have a good book and a mug of hot chocolate these days.'

'What about poor Bruce?' asked Mavis.
She raised her eyebrows and giggled. 'You never see a dead budgie fall out of a cage, love.'
They both laughed. When the last of their washing was folded and bagged the two women left the building. Outside the grey clouds were threating rain.

'Keep that to yourself,' called Julia, as Mavis walked off. 'And don't tell Mur I said anything to you.'

Peter finished his lunch, then turned off the television where he had been watching the lunchtime news. He took some money from his wallet then returned it to his jacket which was hanging on the back of a chair. It should only take him minutes to walk to the ranch and back, but there was always someone ready to delay him with a natter, or in Bert's case, a moan. Ronnie the swan and his growing family had climbed from the water up onto the bank and were basking in the warmth of the afternoon sunshine. Peter gave them a wide berth. Although Ronnie wasn't as aggressive now that the cygnets had got older, you still had to be wary. After buying his electricity card and an ice cream, he chatted to Vernon and Jeb, drank a coffee then wandered back along the pontoon.

He hadn't locked the stern doors when he left but had pushed them to. Now one was wide open. He stopped momentarily before concluding that he couldn't have closed them properly.

'Silly old fool,' he thought. He chuckled, remembering last week when he had put his ham in the washing machine rather than the fridge. Well, they were situated next to each other.

Stepping inside he saw everything was as he had left it. He turned on the radio, filled the kettle then picked up his jacket which was where he had left it on the back of the chair. He always had a spare electricity card which he kept inside his wallet, just in case. Sliding his hand into the inside pocket he felt for his wallet, it wasn't there. He checked the other pockets, took the cushions off the chair and looked underneath it. Slowly combing his fingers through his neatly trimmed grey beard he scanned around the room, checking every surface to see if he had placed it down elsewhere. He checked the bedroom and the toilet although he was sure he hadn't taken it in either room.

'Maybe he had taken it with him,' he thought. After one final glance around the boat he stepped out onto the pontoon to carefully retrace his steps back to the ranch. The grass had recently been cut so any dropped item, particularly a black wallet, would be clearly seen. By the time he reached the wooden building a sickening feeling of anxiety was beginning to ferment inside his stomach.

Inside the ranch he checked around the coffee machine and felt down the side of the sofa, where he had previously been sitting talking to Jeb. Linda asked how much was in the wallet.
He said there was about fifty pounds in cash. She insisted he use the office phone to stop his credit and debit cards. Vernon checked the toilets and the veranda even though he said he hadn't been there.

Linda was concerned. She liked Peter, a decent sensitive man who didn't have an axe to grind, unlike some in the marina who kept the sharpening stone in their back pocket.
That evening she cycled round to see him. Peter turned off the television, put the kettle on and made two mugs of tea. He ripped open a new packet of chocolate biscuits and scattered some on to a plate.

Linda took one and laughed. 'I'm supposed to be dieting.'

'You don't think somebody came onto the boat and took it?' he asked.

She slowly dunked the biscuit in her tea. 'I can't see it; you were only gone for a short time.'

'Well, what about Lewis and Jodie's money, that just disappeared?'

Linda shook her head. 'I know it's worrying, but I would hate to think it's someone in the marina.'

'What about from outside?' he said.

'It's possible, but they would have to be quick,' she replied.

Peter idled drinking his tea. He sighed deeply. 'I don't know what to make of it, it's a bloody mystery, I just don't need this.'

Linda put her hand on his arm. 'It may still turn up.'

She stood up. 'We could involve the police, but they were pretty useless when Lewis and Jodie called them.'

'Waste of time,' he said sadly.

Linda was troubled as she cycled back to the ranch. This was the second theft from a boat in a short time and it had left a bad taste. She decided to send an e-mail reminding people to keep their boats secure, though she didn't want to alarm them. Many were used to leaving their boats unlocked. Somebody had once remarked that living in the marina was like Britain in the fifties when people left their doors open without fear of intruders.

CHAPTER SIX

The Dark Side

The death of Robert Mugabe, the former President of Zimbabwe, though mourned by some, was celebrated by many others worldwide. This wave of elation was more keenly felt by those who had the misfortune to have lived under or witnessed his tyranny.

It was therefore on a small strip of grass in the depth of the English countryside that two people raised a glass of red wine to toast his overdue demise. Karl and his wife Sheila sat at the wooden bench underneath a large sun umbrella. They had been late converts to boating but now enjoyed every moment of it. Of course, there had been teething problems; how to steer the boat and adjusting to the practicalities involved in living on aboard. But with much enthusiasm and help from other boaters they soon overcame these.

Karl and Sheila's story illustrated the diversity of the past and present lives of moorers in the marina. Karl used to manage a big game reserve in Zimbabwe and had written widely on the subject. They both watched as, in the distance, four hot air balloons meandered silently across a cloudless sky. On the grass, plump sausages and hamburgers sizzled over the hot coals on the small picnic barbecue. Sheila re-filled the glasses; Karl turned the meat.

A lone narrowboat, the evening sun glinting off the paintwork, slipped its moorings and headed out for an evening cruise. The skipper waved. His dog barked. Karl smiled to himself.

'Life could be worse.' He put an arm around Sheila, drank from his wine glass and all thoughts of Robert Mugabe were consigned to the bin.

Jimmy and Eva lifted their bums off the seats to mitigate the jarring effects on their lower regions as their orange tandem bumped across the rough track. On their backs were two rucksacks full of produce from their allotment. Reaching the high security gates at the entrance to the marina they tapped in the secret four-digit code. Slowly the five bar gates shuffled open and they went through. Now on a smooth surface their posteriors could return to the saddles without fear of permanent injury. They peddled into the car park in the Canal Side sector. Karl and Shelia's barbecue smelt good, making Jimmy and Eva feel hungry, as they hadn't eaten since midday. They pushed their tandem to the far end of the grass strip near to where their boat was moored. Jimmy padlocked it to a metal post. Eva took the bags into the boat and unpacked them onto a table in the galley.

It had just gone six o'clock when Jimmy banged on the roof of Lewis and Jodie's boat. Lewis came to the door still dressed in his blue suit. He hadn't been in from work long.

After moving down from London, he had been fortunate enough to secure a job with a financial consultant in town. The salary was substantially less than he was earning in the City, but then so was the stress.

Jimmy laughed. 'How's the pox doctor's clerk? Got a minute?' he asked.
They sat on the wooden bench sheltered underneath a large sun umbrella. Lewis removed his jacket and loosened his tie.

'What's up mate?' he asked.

'Did you hear that Peter had his wallet nicked off his boat?'
Lewis nodded. 'So, Jodie was saying.'

'Don't you think it's a bit of a coincidence after Jodie's money going missing. And why is it only happening on this side of the marina?' he asked.
Lewis thought for a moment. 'I suppose so mate, but you can't prove anything.'

'Unless they're caught in the act,' said Jimmy.
Lewis laughed. 'Ok Sherlock, how's that going to happen?'

The third, and by far the most intriguing, of the sectors in the marina was known as the Dark Side. The name conjured up thoughts of evil things, sinister happenings and ghostly apparitions, the latter though, not wholly untrue. Several people had experienced paranormal activity since the marina had been built. The smooth tarmac road surface which commenced at the marina entrance passed the rear of the ranch, fronted the compound then stopped abruptly. Here it reverted to a rough track.

There is some debate as to where the Dark Side begins, and the Ranch Sector ends.
It was generally accepted, though not by all, that the boundary was on the sharp bend by the recently constructed access path to the main road. For those moored close to the assumed demarcation line, this ideological discussion could result in them being left in 'no man's land.'
Not a pleasant outlook, and there was no discount in mooring fees for being 'sector-less'.

The view from the Dark Side was quite exceptional; flat arable fields with trees clustered along low hedgerows at their edge, a winding road that splintered at the junction. Model sized traffic swept along it, beneath blisters of low patchwork hills. On the crest a sun-tinted farmhouse, wisps of grey smoke rising from a tall bricked chimney.

The track continued along the line of pontoons. A low fence bordered the grass verge with signs indicating a steep slope beyond. Whilst there were many boats moored in the Dark Side there were far fewer visible inhabitants than in other sectors. Their illusive comings and goings often contributed to the 'them over there' view expressed by people in the other sectors.

From the small cul-de-sac car park, they could gaze across the waters to the Nordic community of the Canal Side sector. Occasionally a scintilla of polite dialogue was exchanged between the two.

Alex, the warden, stood on the veranda of the ranch and trained his powerful field glasses towards the far side of the marina. Moving them slowly from left to right he scanned the morning landscape of the Dark Side. He was unsure of the objectives, but orders were orders. Regular monitoring had been implemented by the previous marina manager who had always harboured a suspicion of wrongdoing and possible insurgency.

Having served in several war zones, Alex was well used to this long-term surveillance. His trained eye could detect anything out of the ordinary, such as a person carrying a bag of coal in August or parked cars untainted by mud or dust. But by far the greatest challenge were the drones. Operated by a well-known online shopping company they would regularly infiltrate the marina's air space before ejecting their load to the recipients below. Alex had the authority to lock on and destroy, using the small handheld rocket launcher disguised as a set of defibrillators.

Glenda was moored halfway along between the sharp bend and the car park. She threw open the front doors of her narrowboat, Spirit, and breathed in the crisp early morning air. Her black cat, Aura, slid between her legs, jumped across the gunwales onto the pontoon then disappeared down the grassed bank to the field beyond. He would not be seen again until dusk fell, when he would return with a dead rodent and dump it on the front of the boat.

Stepping back inside the boat she took a recently defrosted mouse from a plastic container. Removing the lid of a glass tank she dropped the rodent inside. Boris, her one metre long Python, lay perfectly still in one corner. Only the slow opening of one eye indicated his awareness of breakfast.

'There you are my beauty,' she cackled. 'Eat up.'

She drew back the thick purple curtains before putting the kettle on. Glenda was a spiritual healer and medium. Several boaters, both inside the marina and out on the canal, regularly beat a path to her door to sort out their various physical, psychological and spiritual ailments. Many of these people held the self-belief that they were spiritual, though when asked could never quite explain what this meant. Still if they burned joss sticks, wore beads and chanted, they felt they remained in character.

Glenda lived alone, apart from Aura and Boris. She had been moored on the Dark Side of the marina for three years. Before buying a narrow boat, she had toured the country in an old 'Bongo' van, stopping off at remote campsites and Spiritualist Churches on the way.

Allison wasn't moored on the Dark Side anymore. She had sold her wide beam, Sammy, which had been named after her previous dog, also a German Shepherd. This had been her home since moving down from London some years ago. After the space of a wide beam, downsizing to a sixty-foot new build narrowboat took some getting used to. The advantage being that it was easier to handle and moor up, which was important when you are on your own. Allison didn't do noise or gatherings, so the peaceful ambiance of the Canal Side sector seemed a good choice, and the car park was near to the entrance. A mooring had become available next to Alan and Jock, so she took it.

Glenda had been her neighbour and a good friend who often looked after her dog, Zeke, when she was working. Zeke was a gentle black German shepherd of exceptional size, yet a more passive animal of this breed would be hard to find. Both women were sensitive souls and would often spend an enjoyable evening talking over a bottle of Gordon's gin, with more than a passing interest in EastEnders.

The deep throated bark was like the low thud of a small explosive device. Alan put down his guitar and went to the front of his boat. Zeke's large, black, wolf like head was poking through the stern canopy of Allison's boat.

'What are you barking at, great hound?' said Alan.

Allison came up the steps at the stern. 'He wants his walk with Barney,' she said, attaching the lead to his collar. Zeke stepped gingerly onto the wooden pontoon, his large paws scrambling urgently towards the grass bank. He hated walking on the slated platform. Ronnie, always up for a bit of aggression, had glided silently close to the pontoon and hissed loudly at Zeke as he walked by. Allison shooed him away with a carrier bag.

'Oh, by the way, thanks for the cottage pie,' called Alan, holding up an empty glass dish. 'I'll leave it on the boat.'

Allison waved. 'Glad you enjoyed it.'

Zeke's large canine paws weren't the only ones to tread the sod around the marina. Shadow, a more traditionally coloured and smaller German Shepherd, lived on board the narrowboat, Grey Mist, on the Dark Side. His owner, Terry, was a 'what you see is what you get' sort of person, with a colourful vocabulary, not that this worried him in the slightest.

Before descending the flight of locks to the marina below Terry had enjoyed two seasons moored on the edge of town opposite the old wharf. This recently renovated stretch of towpath ran from the top lock by the main road to the narrow road bridge alongside the wharf. It was a popular place to moor and, in the summer, had a cosmopolitan and festive feel to it. This was further enhanced by beer and music festivals. Passing hire boats, many of whom had overseas visitors on board and were also keen to stop and explore the market town.

Built in 1810 the wharf handled goods such as timber, stone, and grain. There were several bonded warehouses for tobacco and spirits and a corn store. Unfortunately, along with most other canals throughout the country, competition from alternative carriers eventually heralded the end of this way of life.

Sitting with Shadow on the stern of his boat Terry had got to know the regulars and visitors alike. The local dog walkers, clutching poo bags, came morning and night in all weathers, their charges keen to play with Shadow on the towpath, although sometimes the smaller breeds could be intimidated by his size. Then there were the forgotten elderly who had fled the bleakness of four walls with the accompanying deafening silence, to dwell alongside the canal in search of visual or verbal contact with the busy human race. The invisible lonely who, with barely disguised envy, watched as happy families and friends either floated or sauntered by. By lunchtime, stressed office and retail workers arrived seeking a quiet place to eat their lunch and meditate on their lot in life.

Probably the saddest of all, depending on your viewpoint, were the homeless, drug addicts and alcoholics who regularly congregated around a wooden bench whilst consuming endless cans of Special Brew. They had somehow managed to obtain a small aged GRP cruiser without an engine. A small number of the group, who had been camping in the woods behind the cemetery, took up residence on this floating hulk. Inevitably, being unlicensed and not canal worthy it was eventually seized by the authorities and removed from the waterways. The inhabitants, after a brief sortie afloat, no doubt returned to the woods, from whence they came. Terry knew them all. So, it was a sad day for him and Shadow when he decided to leave, but needs must and so he did.

On arrival at the Dark Side, Shadow had struck up a friendship with a small black Staffie called Billie, whose owner, Gordon, was moored on the same pontoon. Being much smaller than Shadow their play could be mistaken for fighting, and indeed some anonymous person, with little else to do, had reported Shadow to Linda for being aggressive, much to the amusement and consternation of Terry. His response to such a charge was let's say 'colourful'.

CHAPTER SEVEN

Pastures New

It was a chill autumnal breeze that greeted the three wise men when they met for their morning coffee outside the ranch building. In deference to the changing weather Jeb had swapped his well-worn shorts for a pair of grey tracksuit bottoms. Judging by the accumulated number of holes in them, they could have been discarded by a welder's mate.

Bert, as usual, complained about the hard, cold benches and the effect they had on his ever-worsening piles. Bruce suggested that if they hurt that much, he should bring a fold up chair from his boat. Jeb laughed and said that if he got in one, he would never get out of it. Bert, not impressed, emitted a loud snort, took out his packet of tobacco and rolled a thin cigarette.

'Can't see the point in that,' said Jeb. 'Two puffs and it's gone.'

Bert complained about the price of tobacco.

Bruce stood up saying he needed the loo. Bert muttered something disparaging about Bruce's prostate. Jeb laid his pipe on the table. Taking a small silver knife from his pocket he proceeded to slowly scrape the inside of the blackened bowl of his pipe, finally tapping the ash into the palm of his hand. Pulling a pipe cleaner from a packet, he gently pushed it into the mouthpiece then withdrew it. Unzipping a soft leather pouch, he took some tobacco and pushed it into the bowl.

'Bloody hell,' said Bert, 'it's like performing an operation, just to have a smoke.'

Jeb was just about to reply when Bruce returned. He was laughing and holding the handle of the door from the men's toilets. 'It just came off in my hand,' he said.

'Vernon only repaired that yesterday,' chuckled Jeb.

'Well, he didn't do a very good job did he?' grumbled Bert.

Jeb held his Zippo lighter to his pipe. 'You better go and give it to him,' he said, striking the flint with his thumb.

'And tell him not to keep bodging things,' shouted Bert.
Jeb breathed a sigh of satisfaction as he exhaled a cloud of grey smoke and blew it into the air.

Bruce returned with thee more coffees.

'What did he say?' asked Jeb.

'He wasn't there. I gave it to Linda,' he replied. 'She can give it to him.'

The three men sat quietly for a moment watching as Ronnie the swan and his family climbed awkwardly from the water and waddled up onto the bank. Horace, the resident heron, stood poised on the end of a jetty watching as the unsuspecting shadows of small fish passed beneath him. On the crest of the grassed bank that ran alongside the road a woman walked three dogs, all determined to pull her in different directions.

'Can't see the point in having three dogs on a boat,' said Bert.

'Maybe she's on her own,' replied Bruce. 'They keep her company.'

'Well, Jeb's on his own, he hasn't got three dogs has he?'

Jeb inhaled the last of the smoke from his morning pipe. 'I'm not really an animal person, I wouldn't have the patience.'

'Nor would I,' said Bert.

'Well, there's a surprise,' replied Bruce.

'We 'ad chickens when I was a kid,' said Bert, 'but my old man came home drunk one night and wrung all their necks. The next day, when he'd sobered up, 'e wanted to know who had killed them. We never got any more after that.'

They both laughed.

'I could have a goldfish,' said Jeb, 'they're low maintainace, then when I'm fed up with watching it swim round and round, I could throw it in the canal.'

Bert chuckled. 'Don't do that, you'll 'ave all the do-gooders after you on that Twitter thing.'

Bruce said. 'I nearly knocked one over once.'

'What, a goldfish?' laughed Bert.

Bruce smiled. 'No. Some silly girl staring at her phone stepped into the road in front of me. I had to swerve to miss her.'

'Bloody morons, I don't understand it,' replied Bert. 'It's a bloody obsession, and it's not just kids. You see adults in pubs and cafés, eyes glued to the damn things, like Zombies'.

'It's certainly stifled interaction,' said Jeb. Again, Bert chuckled. 'It's probably stifled intercourse as well.'

'That's no bad thing,' offered up Bruce. 'It might help reduce the world population.'

Vernon, looking like a mortician's assistant, arrived wearing wellington boots and yellow rubber gloves, in his hand a long piece of wire and a length of hose.

'Anybody for colonic irrigation?' he shouted.

'Is it any good for piles?' asked Bert.

'Perfect,' replied Vernon. 'Do you wanna try? Bend over.'

Bruce laughed. 'He might enjoy it.'

'What's happened?' asked Jeb.

'The bloody toilets have backed up again,' he said irritably. 'Someone's been putting wipes down them. We keep telling people, but they don't listen.' Bruce asked if he wanted some help. He declined saying it shouldn't take long.

'Don't fall in,' called Bert, as he disappeared around the corner.

They watched in silence as a boater fed the carp from the stern of his boat.

'They're big buggers in there,' said Bruce. Jeb threw the last of his cold coffee onto the gravel. 'I'm leaving the marina in the spring,' he said. Bruce and Bert looked at each other, slightly shocked at the suddenness of the announcement.

'What?' asked Bert abruptly, unsure if he had heard him correctly.

'Time for pastures new,' Jeb said.

Bert shifted his position on the hard seat. 'What pastures. Where?'

Jeb had been dreading this day. He had made the decision some weeks ago and was just waiting for the right time to tell them, but of course there never was one. He knew his old friends would be disappointed, after all they had known each other a long time and were often referred to as the marina's version of 'Last of the Summer Wine'

'A new marina near Milton Keynes,' Jeb replied to Bert's question.

'But why?' asked Bruce. 'You know everybody here, you're settled, part of the furniture.'

Jeb fiddled with his pipe. 'Well that's just it. I'm too settled, same old, same old, every day. My life's going nowhere fast. I just need to do something different before I shuffle off this mortal coil.'

'Christ,' replied Bruce, 'that's pretty deep.'

Jeb stood up. 'How about another coffee?'

Bert grumbled, 'I need a strong one after that bloody revelation.'

Bruce said, 'I hope he has thought this through. It's a big move to make.'

Bert rolled one of his wafer-thin cigarettes. 'It's a bloody long way to go for some soul searching.'

Jeb arrived back with three strong coffees and a packet of Eccles cakes.

'A little treat,' he said. 'I got them before Hazel came in or there wouldn't be any left.'

'What about all the locks?' asked Bruce. 'There's going to be a lot.'

Jeb bit into the Eccles cake then produced a piece of paper from his pocket.

'158 locks, 39 movable bridges, 11 small aqueducts and 3 tunnels,' he said, taking a sip of coffee from the mug. 'I'll just take me time. I've got all summer.'

Bert snorted. 'You'll need the next bloody summer as well, that's if you don't die in the process.'

'Have you told Linda and Vernon?' asked Bruce.

Jeb said he hadn't yet. But he would be giving them three months' notice.

He knew though that telling other people wouldn't be required, as once Bert got back to his boat and told his wife Mur, it would soon be round the marina. As if by telepathy he saw her come walking down the pontoon taking a basket full of washing to be dried. Bert, true to form, called her over. 'Guess what Mur?' he said.

Before pumpkins appeared in the shops those who had intended to return to the marina after the summer, had already done so. Some had slipped serenely away in the spring, others left to a more boisterous farewell. Interestingly the style of their departure often matched the nature of their character on shore.

For the more adventurous, their exploration would take them beyond their home canal and onto the supine waters of the upper stretches of the Thames. Depending then on their navigable desire they could continue onwards towards the Oxford canal and beyond, or head on downstream towards Teddington. Either way this experience qualified them to rid themselves of the name 'ditch crawlers.' This term was often associated with narrowboat owners, but now they could forever claim to have cruised the wide majestic waters of the River Thames.

The more seasoned boater may well have opted to drop below Teddington Lock and onto the tidal flow. This scenic stretch would take them through the Richmond half lock before turning into the tidal lock at Brentford, then continuing up the Grand Union. Others may choose to carry on down the Thames to Limehouse Lock, though navigating the pool of London was not for the faint hearted. Often these boaters would beat a path to Jimmy's door for advice on tidal cruising.

After their short or lengthy journeying on the network, their return to the marina often mirrored that of their departure. Some arriving quietly and dignified, others theatrical and noisy.

Our three wise men had between them, over the years, amassed a considerable amount of boating hours on which they often reminisced, but generally felt little desire to travel and replicate them. None would admit it, but the body just wasn't as nimble as before, so they restricted their travelling to a few miles either side of the marina and of course regular cruises to the local pubs. That was until Jeb had decided to up anchor and move on.

A weak sun had broken through the morning chill. Jeb, Bert, and Bruce were on their third mug of coffee. Mur had delivered some warm, freshly made ships biscuits to the table. Bert asked her if she could fetch him a cushion. She called him a lazy sod but fetched it for him anyway. Bert didn't mind being called lazy or impatient. He knew it was true. He maintained it was an entitlement that came with age.

There was the now familiar sound of spittle being sucked through the stem of Jeb's pipe. He coughed loudly and laid it on the table.

'Thought you were giving that thing up?' asked Bruce.

Jeb chuckled. 'I'm trying,' he said, preparing the bowl for another re-fill of tobacco.

Bert said, 'You carry on coughing like that, it'll be you giving up first.'

Jeb laughed. 'Well, you've got to die of something.'

The intermittent noise of the horn was soft at first, barely audible, then growing louder as the boat progressed slowly under the lift bridge and into the marina basin. Bert jumped up to see what it was. 'Oh, Christ! They're back, the bloody peace is shattered,' he said.

The other two stood to see who he was talking about. Several of the incoming boater's friends were waving and calling from the end of the pontoon on the Canal Side sector.

Bert grumbled loudly. 'Six months peace we've had. Look at 'em, it's like the return of the fleet from the bloody Falklands.'

Bruce and Jeb watched as the boat slowed before turning and attempting to reverse between a moored boat and the pontoon. The woman wearing a silly hat stood on the bow, her arms raised like a triumphant boxer who has just performed a stunning knockout. The reception party shouted inane comments across the water, none of which she could hear above the noise of the over revving engine. Bert groaned. The steerer, through fatigue or distraction was struggling to place the stern end alongside the pontoon.

Bert shouted in exasperation. 'Give it some wellie man.'

The steerer waved to him, convinced that he was happy to see them return. Bert sat down shaking his head in frustration. 'They never give it enough wellie. And what's he wearing that bloody bowler for?'

Bruce picked up his cup, throwing the last of his cold coffee onto the gravelled surface.

'He's probably got a beer mug hanging from his belt as well,' he laughed.

Jeb stood up. 'Time for some breakfast I think.' He went into the ranch to buy some eggs and bacon. Bert followed him, stretching and rubbing his cold bum as he wandered slowly along the pontoon towards his boat.

Dusk had fallen across the fields when the small white van turned off the main road onto the track that led to the marina entrance. The driver slowed and stopped momentarily on the bend by the old barn. The machinery which once was used for agricultural production, now rusting beneath a creaky corrugated roof. Opposite, a stile led through a field to the canal and the bottom lock of the flight. He rolled slowly down the hill past the tall metal fencing that fronted the slipway next to the bubble. The plain sided van did not pass through the gates, but instead parked on a large stony area adjacent to the marina entrance. Nearby a narrowboat weathered by the previous season sat on a long trailer waiting to have its hull blacked.

The driver, a young man in his late twenties, stepped out and relieved himself at the edge of the field. He wore a torn black tee shirt, camouflage-coloured trousers and a pair of beaten-up trainers. This was in stark contrast to two earlier visits to the marina, when, wearing smart casual clothes he had wandered around unchallenged. In the unlikely event that he was questioned, a prepared story would be forthcoming; a friend in Oxford was looking for a mooring and had asked him to visit the marina and he was just on his way to the office to check availability and prices.

He went to the back of the van and opened the doors. The rear offside light was held in place with thick adhesive tape. Inside, was a narrow mattress with a rolled up sleeping bag. Next to it a bowl for washing and a water carrier. He climbed in and closed the doors behind him. Reaching into a supermarket carrier bag he opened a can of beer, took out his phone then lay back on the mattress.

CHAPTER EIGHT

Winter Looms

Its arrival is gradual, stealth-like. For the boaters and dwellers in Crockenhill Marina the coming of autumn 'the season of mists' is a subtle almost unnoticed event, as the breath of an ebbing summer becomes tinged with a chilled edge. Soon the glossy backdrop of sun kissed boats and reflective waters will be brushed to a matt finish. Like confetti the paths and tracks will be littered with a carpet of fallen leaves. *'Love the trees until their leaves fall off, then encourage them to try again next year.' (Chad Sugg)*

The more observant will have noticed swallows and house martins starting their migration down to warmer climes. And where do the Canadian geese go?

The first needles of grey smoke appear from recently redundant chimneys, stoked by the thin blooded and 'not so hardy' boaters. In the ranch an occasional bag of coal and sack of kindling sit forlornly and unwanted against a featureless wall. Most customers pass by without a glance, not wishing to contemplate the forthcoming inclement weather and increased cost of living.

For those with an interest in maintaining the exterior of their boat, and some aren't, it's a last-minute scramble to finish the 'must do' jobs. The lazy, or permanently nagged, can now blame the onset of winter for their reluctance to finish the work they started three months ago. Inevitably as the October clock ticks towards an end a veil of early darkness descends across the land.

This prompts the recent phenomenon of head torches. Small white beams elevated between five and six feet from the ground, which to an approaching individual can appear as a ghostly 'orb' hovering and bobbing in the darkness. As the working boats of yesteryear often carried coal it should be of little surprise that present day boaters should wish to emulate the appearance of a miner, though less 'trendy' folk still hold a torch in their hand, or if both are required grip it in their teeth.

The ancient and annual Celtic festival of Samhain, where people dress up to ward off evil spirits, is one of several events staged in October at the ranch building. Grotesque 'Jack o' Lantern' pumpkins which, thanks to America, have replaced turnips, adorn windowsills and tables. The revellers intent on invoking the dark arts cavort about in cheap online or homemade costumes and masks. But, beware. Beyond the heavy mix of witches' brew and erotic rhythm, the ghouls await ready to snatch the souls of the wandering inebriated, or sexual deviant.

As for trick and treat, the marina is barren when it comes to children, which makes the sign on entering the marina even more baffling. 'Slow down 10mph. Children playing.' Where?
Of course, there are those who will say 'thank god for that', our three wise men being amongst them.

But as Jimmy and Eva often pointed out to anyone who asked. 'Do we really want the marinas to become floating retirement homes.'

Jimmy had told Bert that he had read the average age of a boat owner is forty-eight. He had shrugged with complete indifference. Eva though, always ready to bait him said,

'You never know Bert. With time and a little nautical nookie, the road sign might become relevant.'

He shook his head. 'That's all we need, lots of snotty nosed kids running around the place.'

Jimmy patted him on the head. 'You old coffin dodger,' he laughed.

Lennie sat with Peter outside the ranch scrapping green paint from his bare legs. The colour of a boat he had been painting. Alan, fresh from purgatory in one of the town's supermarkets, joined them.

'Poor old Guy Fawkes,' Lennie said suddenly. 'Nobody lights a beacon to his plight. Not even the Roman Catholics whose cause he was promoting. Hung, drawn and quartered, or at least he would have been if he hadn't fallen off the scaffold and broken his neck beforehand.

Peter laughed. 'Well he did try to blow up the House of Lords.'

'Good on him,' replied Lennie. 'Shame someone doesn't try it today.'

Alan agreed. 'Bloody old duffers, it should be abolished. Three hundred quid a day they get, and what do they do for it?'

Lennie continued. 'There was hardly a bang in the marina this year, not even a bloody sparkler.'

'It's the health and safety police,' said Peter. Lennie stood up laughing. 'Stuff 'em. Let's 'ave some fun next year; a few Chinese crackers and bangers.'

Peter chuckled. 'That'll make Vernon hop about a bit sharpish.'

'And a few Catherine wheels pinned to the loo doors?' added Alan.

'You got it mate,' said Lennie, jumping on his bike and cycling off to finish the paint job.

As the heady month of December arrives, the occasional bag of coal in the ranch building has become a tall mound of bagged sedimentary rock. Shelves labour under the weight of boxes of firelighters. Now the 'not so hardy, are joined by the 'pretty hardy' in needing to warm, or over warm the interior of their floating homestead. The subsequent effect is a pall of grey smoke hanging across an already depressed and murky sky. Another indicator of the fall in temperature is the disappearance of much-loved summer shorts. Though to be fair not by all.

The keener exposers of human flesh hold out until the snow is deep enough to chill the kneecaps. Only then are the jeans reluctantly dragged from the rear of the drawer.

If you do not have the ice-skating skills of Torvil and Dean, it is a wise to adopt the 'Penguin wobble' when navigating the slippery pontoons.

The open-air communal sector gatherings are long gone. Now boaters either hunker down in their 'steel tubes' or seek like-minded discussion in the ranch building, which in all fairness does cater for all types and eccentricities, even those wearing shorts and a tee shirt when it's bloody freezing.

Our three wise men had differing views on the forthcoming festive period. Bert loathed it with a vengeance and woe betide anyone who directed a Ho! Ho! Ho! towards him. Bruce embraced it, and Jeb couldn't give a fig, which just about summed up the view of the nation, along with that other contentious issue, Brexit.

In the ranch building stood the obligatory artificial plastic Christmas tree accompanied by a string of flashing coloured lights snaking across the ceiling. A worthy attempt at evoking the Xmas spirit, though giving the impression of the reception area of a Travel Lodge hotel.

Across the dark expanse of the marina the illumination of boats was, compared to previous years, a spartan affair, with boat owners either absent or preferring austerity to flashing glitter and heavier electricity usage. Bruce, who had decorated his boat, suggested that Bert might do the same. The reply was distinctly unseasonal.

That said, boaters are in the main a jolly, communal lot and the moorers in Crockenhill Marina were no exception to this. Of course, you had a few miserable malcontents, but they were in the minority. Above all they were pragmatic folk.

As that famous philosopher Arnold Gutterbucket once said, 'Romantics make for fair weather sailors.'

Despite his outward appearance to the contrary, Jeb was an intelligent and engaging conversationalist, raising topics with his peers that might otherwise be considered too highbrow. To quote but a few:

'What afternoon did they show the Wooden Tops and Rag Tag and Bobtail?

'How many pints in an eight-pint container?

'Is it the River Avon or the Avon River?

'Who would you shoot first if you had a firing squad at your disposal?

The eclectic mix of characters in the marina did at times prompt a more in-depth serious discussion, fuelled of course by copious amounts of alcohol. Politics and religion were generally given a wide berth. Sex, in all its guises and perversions was occasionally raised, though few could remember with much clarity their last heady experiences of the flesh. This often brought the discussion nicely round to erectile disfunction, enlarged prostates and the frequency with which one should check their testicles.

The wives and partners tended to group themselves together, away from the increasing volume and opinions of their spouses. An occasional shake of the head or raised eyebrow said it all. There were of course exceptions to this who enjoyed slashing their sabre with the rest of them and did it with great gusto.

Similar discussions took place in the other areas of the marina. The Canal Side sector had two distinct groups who congregated at each end of the narrow grass strip. Their earthy exchanges were less 'scatty', or to be polite, 'wide ranging' than those of the people in the Ranch Sector. Stimulated by the 'not so occasional' tipple, these multifarious individuals preferred a more fluid dialogue. The smaller grouping at the car park end, opposite the drab looking chalets, included Karl and Sheila. A passing fly landing amongst this convivial tribe would have discovered a diet of topical conversation, albeit at times with a localised critique.

CHAPTER NINE

Tangled web

Without diverting her gaze from the smart phone which she held in her left hand, Hazel took another bite from the giant Eccles cake that she had been slowly consuming for the last five minutes. A white mug filled with a second strong coffee stood in front of her on the round wooden table. The rhythmic cockney voices of Chas and Dave drifted from the radio on the shelf by the tinned vegetables. Hazel was a round jolly sort of person, not extravert, but thoughtful and caring.

It was unusually quiet in the ranch building that late afternoon. Her distant ruminations were disturbed only by the occasional incoming phone call to the office where Linda, the marina manager, sat transfixed in front of the computer screen. Looking out across a dank marina, Hazel's thoughts drifted back to that early summer's day when she and partner Sid had readied themselves for a three-month cruise into the unknown. There was of course trepidation at the thought of doing battle with the elements; the unpredictability of the English weather, broken lock gates, water shortage, fouled propellers, etc, etc.

Recent months had been a challenging time for them both and remaining in the marina would have been the easy option, offering them safety and convenience. But when at last the day of departure arrived, the symbolic act of releasing the lines that tethered them to the pontoon left few doubts in their minds as to the validity of their decision.

Like Christopher Columbus before them, they bade farewell to friends and family and embarked on a pilgrimage of adventure and exploration. Passing under the lift bridge at the entrance to the marina, a huge wave of relief and freedom engulfed them. Like all souls who venture warily from their comfort zone into that swirling void beyond, the discovery of one's self becomes as important as the journey undertaken. Hazel and Sid would be no exception to this.

After many weeks of toil and sweat, and the occasional mutiny by a crew member, they washed up on the shores of Bucking- ham -shire. Otherwise known as the (scire) of Bucca's home. Here they were cautiously met by the inhabitants of Middleton, a small hamlet on the river Ouzel. The indigenous natives of this marshy terrain were at first suspicious of the newcomers with their strange West Country accents and weathered appearance. This soon subsided though when Hazel and Sid stepped ashore and, as a peace offering, produced a box full to the brim with giant Eccles cakes. This sugary treat was previously unknown to the omnivores of Middleton and they embraced it without a thought to forthcoming tooth decay.

Trust and friendship were soon established between them and they in turn were gifted a sacred paper mâché cow. This was a great honour, though whilst gratefully received it did present a storage problem on their narrowboat during the homeward journey. But as they say, 'Never look a gift cow in the mouth'.

Hazel was jolted back to the present by a sudden blast of air from the opened door.
Peter, looking world weary, stepped into the room and slumped into a chair next to her.

'Alright darling?' she asked.
He clearly wasn't, complaining bitterly that there were dog's hairs in the tumble drier.

'Maybe somebody shampooed their mut,' she said, laughing. It was a loud infectious guffaw that reverberated around the pine panelled walls. Peter wasn't for pacifying, he stood up and headed for the coffee machine. 'I need a woman who does,' he called, without turning around.

'Don't look at me darling,' she said. 'I don't do. I just offer psychological support.'

That made him smile. 'Any bloody support would be welcome right now.'

She guessed that as usual he had little on the boat to eat. It wasn't that he couldn't afford it, he just lost the will to live the moment he stepped into a supermarket. Who could blame him?

'We're going shopping soon love, would you like me to collect something for you?' she asked.

He sat back down with his coffee. 'No, I'm fine thanks.'

'What did you have for breakfast, Peter?' she asked.

'Cornflakes,' he replied, taking a large gulp from the cup.
She continued. 'What about lunch?'

He gave a wry smile. 'Cornflakes.'

Hazel shook her head. 'And dinner tonight?'

'Don't ask,' he replied laughing.

The last of the coffee was drained from the mug. 'Better get going,' he said, moving towards the door.

Hazel smiled, 'See you soon love.'

A few people had come and gone during their discussion in the ranch. One remained. Hazel didn't know him. Maybe he was from the Dark Side; they tended to keep themselves to themselves over there. He smiled as he left with a ready meal from the freezer and a selection of DVD's.

A black veil was falling across the expanse of the marina. How she disliked the early winter darkness and forced hibernation. She longed for the summer to arrive. She and Sid were already planning another cruise. This time, their exploration would take them further afield to the little-known Midlands and beyond. Outside, a cold chill blew in from the water's edge. She shivered and pulled her wrap tight across her chest. It was time to return to the boat and play the housewife. Sid would want his dinner.

Lennie, Peter, Jeb and a few of the usual suspects had gathered on the veranda for a beer. She waved before stepping from the gravel surface onto the wooden pontoon. Vernon had recently cleaned it so it shouldn't be as slippery as before. The unmistakable smell of coal burning stoves laced the air. Overhead the first of the night sky diamonds were peppering the blackness.

It would be a cold night, and a frosty morning.

After Hazel had left the ranch, Linda pulled down the window blinds and closed the door. She was tired and just wanted to go back to their boat, kick her shoes off and relax. Vernon had gone ahead to light the fire so it should be nice and cosy for when she arrived. She sat down on one of the sofas, just for a moment, to gather her thoughts. It was rare for her to have the opportunity of some quiet time. She watched as a small spider sat motionless in the centre of a recently spun web, no doubt waiting for an unsuspecting fly to arrive. She mused at the fragility of the fine silky substance.

It reminded her of the tangled web that we weave for ourselves as we navigate the oceans of life. Those special relationships that were meant to last forever, but didn't, then dwindled and faded away. The many turnings missed, or signposts not seen or ignored. And the regrets, oh, the regrets. That deep pool of 'if only,' which always rises to the surface and catches you off guard when the band plays that favourite song.

Of course, there were, and are, good times too, happy and joyful occasions that are stored forever in the long-term memory. She felt a small lump start to form in the back of her throat. Standing up she patted the cushion before replacing it onto the sofa. 'Doesn't do to dwell,' she thought, replacing her convivial mask.

Outside on the veranda the chilled group were laughing at the unfortunate guy who had moved his boat without unplugging the electricity cable from the pod. An expensive mistake to make. Although they all conceded it was easily done.

Jeb said; 'The man who never makes mistakes has never made anything.'

'Have you seen that white van parked by the entrance?' Lennie asked the others. They hadn't, although Gerry who like Lennie was sporting a recent 'Peaky Blinders' haircut, had seen a young chap hanging around. Jeb thought it could just be some homeless bloke living in his van.

Gerry took a puff on his cigarette. 'Why there though?' he asked.

Jeb shrugged. 'Why not, they've got to go somewhere?'

Lennie wasn't convinced with that explanation. 'I'll have a look tomorrow when I take the dog for a walk. Now I'm going back to the boat, it's bloody freezing.'

Jeb chuckled. 'You need to get rid of those shorts mate.'

Lennie left the veranda with a single finger gesture directed towards him.

Jeb laughed out loud. 'And you.'

Linda turned the lights off in the building and locked the door. Walking around the corner she was surprised to see them still huddled together on the veranda. 'You boys still here?' she said, laughing.

'Last puff,' replied Jeb. He took a small penknife from his Parker jacket and scraped the ash from the bowl of his pipe.

'See that?' said Gerry, pointing skywards. 'A shooting star.'

Peter finished off his bottle of red wine. 'You can often see the satellites going over when it's clear like this.'

Jeb flicked his Zippo and held the long orange flame to his pipe. He stood looking up into the bespangled heavens above. 'It's amazing when you think that the nearest star 'Proxima Centauri' is 4.3 light years away from earth.'

Gerry and Peter exchanged a bemused glance.

'Yes right,' laughed Peter. 'We knew that.'

Jeb continued. 'We're lucky here. Because of light pollution our solar system is no longer visible to 77 % of the UK population.'

Gerry chuckled. 'Ok Patrick Moore, I'm off to bed.'

Lennie woke early, he always did. Throwing on a pair of shorts and a coat, he called his little brown and white terrier, Toby, then left the boat. Outside the retreating darkness was still lingering over the new day. He could hear the noise of the increasing traffic as it swept by on the fast road into town. There was a loud crash as the paladin containing discarded glass was wheeled from the compound and hoisted into the back of a waiting lorry. Apart from the toilet lights the ranch was in darkness, as were most of the boats.

He went along the grass bank at the side of the access road, stopping occasionally to let the little dog relieve itself. Reaching the entrance to the marina he pressed the green button to open the high security gates. The white van was still parked where he had seen it previously. Walking close to the parked vehicle he was aware of the noise from his tread on the loose stones. He didn't want to disturb the possible occupant. The darkness had dispersed enough to enable him to see through the front windows of the van. Apart from a discarded beer can and empty cigarette packet the stained front seats were empty. He went to the back of the vehicle. Two black pieces of cloth acting as curtains covered the rear windows making observation inside impossible. Lennie put his ear close to the side of the van. Nothing. If anybody was inside, he was either in a deep sleep or dead.

He chuckled. If it was the latter, it would at least offer some excitement for the people in the marina, whose lives could otherwise be quite mundane.

Carefully he walked away across the stones until he reached the edge of the field beyond, where he unclipped the dog's lead and let him run free. Gently inclining, he followed the path at the perimeter of the waterlogged field. He threw a stick and the little terrier scampered through the muddy puddles to retrieve it. He always did.

Reaching the ridge, it afforded him a good view of the marina and the canal beyond. He stopped, gave the dog a treat, leant on the fence and took his vape from his pocket. He liked it here; he could think and try to make sense of the troubled world and the people who inhabit it.

He checked his watch. A busy day painting boats in the bubble loomed ahead of him. Several cars and vans, their lights piercing the gloom, were leaving the marina, the occupants no doubt heading for work. Reaching the bottom of the field he gave one more glance at the white van, before walking back through the gate. He waved as Jimmy drove past on his way out of the marina.

CHAPTER TEN

Trust Betrayed

The framed picture was prominently displayed on a small wooden table in the saloon of the sixty-foot narrowboat, Leo, named after their beloved chocolate coloured Labrador, who had died of old age. The image showed them both, husband and wife, standing proudly with their two young children in front of the recently purchased boat. The year was 1985. It was the same boat on which she now stood looking at the slightly faded photograph.

'Where had all the time gone?' she thought to herself whilst wiping the dust from the wooden frame. They were both working then and the children, a boy and girl, were at the local school so cruises were restricted to weekends and holidays. These were mainly on the Trent and Mersey where the boat was moored in Long Eaton, a short distance from their home in Derby.

Their long-awaited retirement in 2010 however afforded them the opportunity to indulge their passion to explore the waterways further afield. After some discussions with their now grown up children it was decided to rent out, rather than sell, the three-bedroom family home in case it didn't work out and they could return. It was a bright and warm day in 2011 when they left the moorings in Long Eaton and embarked on their adventure of a lifetime. The Canal and River Trust termed them 'constant cruisers' though they preferred the name 'water nomads.' Heading up country they criss crossed the system from the Rippon canal in the North, to Liverpool and Llangollen, then across to the Wash in the East. In winter they would check into a marina then leave again in the spring.

Unfortunately, they had an enforced and wasted year moored at a marina close to a hospital in Manchester. He often used to joke that, 'just because I need to keep having a pee, doesn't mean there's anything wrong.' It did, and there was. The doctor's words, 'You should have had it checked earlier,' haunted him to this day. The diagnosis when it came was raw. It was prostate cancer. The shock for both of them and the subsequent treatment was intense. It was only after receiving the all clear twelve months later that she tearfully revealed her fears of losing him.

It took eight years for them to travel south, although they had ventured onto the Oxford Canal once, when visiting friends in Banbury. After calling into Crockenhill Marina to stock up with gas, coal and diesel, they moored a short distance away, near to a footpath that led through fields to a distant village. How they wished they still had Leo. He would have loved the walks. Often, they had discussed getting another dog, but never seemed to get around to it.

There had been a lot of locks to work through lately, so they decided to stay moored alongside the towpath for a few days. It would also give them the opportunity to stock up on provisions from the local town. After a good night's sleep, they breakfasted on bacon and eggs, before unloading their cycles from the roof, and headed into town. It was like many so called Market Towns that they had visited around the country, now shadows of their former selves. Cafés and charity shops dominated the High Street, with the occasional butcher and baker thrown in, most though driven out of business by the large supermarket chains.

However they had learnt, after many visits to similar places, to delve beyond the immediate facade and search out the often-rich history of the town and its past inhabitants. This one was no exception, and they spent an enjoyable two hours visiting the town's museum and castle.

They bought some bread and cakes from the local bakery, but quickly realised that if they were going to complete their shopping list, they had no alternative but to seek out one of the gargantuan purveyors of 'retail therapy.' This they eventually found as usual on the outskirts, sitting like a huge monster, sucking the lifeblood out of the town. Shopping in these places was never a pleasant experience but needs must, and so as Churchill said; 'Keep buggering on.' So they did.

On the return journey to the boat, with their panniers full of a week's shopping, they stopped at an independent coffee shop on the side of the canal. Outside, their bikes had been left unlocked and leaning against a wall, something they would never have contemplated in some of the larger towns that they had visited. Through the window of the coffee shop they watched as two narrowboats passed by on their way to the top of the flight with its many locks.

Neither admitted it but they were now in the autumn of their years and had of late felt the strain, particularly with some of the more stubborn locks and swing bridges. Even the children had started to drop subtle hints, particularly after his cancer scare. But the thought of having to give up this cherished lifestyle was unthinkable. What would they do instead, return to the detached house in Derby and sit looking at four walls, waiting for the grim reaper to call?

Standing up to leave, they recognised a couple who they had seen previously at Crockenhill Marina. They spoke for a few minutes introducing themselves as Bruce and Julia. Outside, the bikes and their cargo were still there, leaning lazily against the low brick wall.

He laughed, 'Told you they would still be here. You can trust people in places like this'.

She smiled, still a little unconvinced.

They took their time cycling back to the boat. There was no hurry. It was chilly but they were well wrapped up. Instead of using the towpath they decided to follow the winding lanes. At a junction a signpost pointed to a local village with a fifteenth century Norman church. They decided to explore. Inside an elderly lady replacing the flowers offered to give them a guided tour of the ancient building. Whilst gratefully received it took a little longer than they had anticipated.

It was mid-afternoon when they pushed open the wooden gate that led from the road onto the towpath. It was only a short distance to where their boat was moored and they were both in need of a refreshing cup of tea and a sandwich. It was the cratch cover that first alerted them. They never left it open, unless they were on the boat, and yet there it was unzipped and flapping about in the breeze. Cautiously he stepped into the bow well, she followed. The wooden front doors had been forced open, hanging limply on their hinges. The inside of the cosy well-ordered boat had been turned upside down. Cupboards had been opened and rifled through, and drawers searched. DVD's and CD's were scattered on the wooden floor, along with documents removed from the small pine desk.

Looking around the compact cabin he could see that the television and both laptops were missing. Fortunately, they had taken their mobile phones into town with them. Bending down she picked up the framed family photograph that she had been looking at earlier in the day. The glass was cracked in several places. A dual emotion of anger and sadness swept through her. She sat down on the sofa and shook her head in disbelief.

'Of all the places they had visited in the country why here?'
He put a comforting hand on her shoulder as she dabbed her eyes.

'Best not touch anything love, until the police come,' he said, gently. 'Fingerprints and all that.'

She stood up and walked through to the bedroom which was at the stern of the boat. The small wardrobe doors had been opened and its contents roughly emptied onto the floor. Her initial instinct was to pick them up and put them away, but instead she left them in an untidy heap and returned to the saloon. He told her that the envelope containing their emergency cash had also been taken from the desk.

Taking his mobile from his pocket he went out onto the towpath and phoned the police. She was going to make some tea for them both but couldn't face the mess in the galley where the cupboards had been searched. A bag of flour had been broken open and spread across the worksurface. She muttered to herself, 'What did they expect to find in there?'

She joined him on the towpath. Finishing the call, he said the police were very busy and the response time could be up to four hours. She sighed.

'So, what do we do now then?'

He returned the phone to his coat pocket and thought for a moment.

'Let's zip up the cratch cover and we'll walk back to the marina. I noticed a tea and coffee machine in the building, and at least it'll be warm.'

She smiled. 'I think we need something stronger.'

'Maybe later love,' he said, taking her hand. She was shivering. He wasn't sure if it was cold or shock. He gave her a hug.

After returning their bikes to the roof and securing them with a padlock, they walked back towards the bridge near the wooden gate then crossed a small grassed field. Beyond the style at the edge was a rough track which led to Crockenhill Marina entrance. The high security gate was open, so they went through.

When Alexandre Dumas wrote 'The Three Musketeers', the phrase he used, 'All for one and one for all,' could have referred to the boating community as well. For in the main, and there are exceptions, they are quick to rally should one of their own be in trouble. So, it was little surprise that our two victims of canal side robbery were met with genuine empathy and concern for their plight.

Linda sat them down and made them both hot drinks. Vernon suggested that they bring the boat into the marina, if only until they got the front doors repaired. They were both hesitant at first but agreed it was for the best. Outside the light was failing fast. Vernon offered to help him fetch the boat. As there was no winding hole, they would have to reverse to the marina entrance, which included going stern first through the lock. She stayed with Linda in the warm building.

After her husband and Vernon had left, Linda rang the police to give them a change of location, when they eventually turned up.

Wilf parked the red Jaguar behind the ranch and stepped out.

'Nice motor,' called Jeb exiting the toilet. 'Alright for some!'

He laughed. 'Not mine, just giving it a service.' Wilf was a motor mechanic who ran his own business and moored his narrowboat, Pirate, on the canal side sector. A big man in stature he was a kind and complex soul, who bore life's kicking's with grace. He opened the boot and took out an empty gas bottle, which he left by the door of the ranch for Vernon to replace, then went inside. Grabbing a coffee, he sat at a nearby table and very soon became aware of the plight of the unfortunate couple opposite him. He followed Linda into the office.

'That's three now,' he said. First Lewis and Jodie, then Peter, now this.
She shook her head. 'I know, but we mustn't jump to conclusions. I still can't believe it's someone in the marina.'

'I don't think it is,' he replied. He closed the office door and told her about the white van parked just outside the marina entrance.

She thought for a moment, 'I haven't seen it, though Lennie did say something about it.'

'You wouldn't,' he said. 'It's around the corner, behind the bushes.'

'How long has it been there?' she asked.
He shrugged. 'Not sure, it comes and goes, but it's a coincidence, don't you think?'
She nodded. 'I do. We must tell the police.'

Wilf sighed. From past experience he had little faith in the old bill. 'What are they going to do? They're not going to keep watch for a van that may or may not turn up and theft, particularly this type, is way down on their agenda. They're too busy investigating hate crimes.'

Linda agreed. It was over four hours since the robbery and they still hadn't arrived.

'So, what do we do then? she asked.

He stood up. 'I'll go down and see if the van is still parked there. Then I need to go and see Alan.'

'Why Alan? she asked.

He gave a wry smile. 'Who better to help catch this bloke?'

She laughed. 'It may be a woman.'

'You never know,' he called. And with that he was gone.

Walking back towards his boat, a pair of headlights appeared from the bend at the top of the track. It was the police. They drew level with him, wound the window down and asked where the office was. He told them and they drove in, the high security gates closing behind them. Wilf waited until they were out of sight then walked round to the shingle patch behind the hedge. As he had anticipated the white van had gone.

He knew Alan was on his boat as he could hear the strumming of his electric guitar from inside. Next door Allison was closing her boat down for the night. Zeke, his large wolf-like head poking through the cover, barked loudly when he saw Wilf approaching.

He jumped. 'Jesus! I didn't see him. Just as well I wasn't breaking in.'

Allison laughed. 'He'd lick you to death.'

Alan opened a bottle of red wine and placed two glasses on the table. Wilf told him about the latest burglary from the boat on the towpath, and his suspicions of the occupant in the white van. Alan was concerned, he had seen how upset Jodie was when her money was stolen.

'Did you tell Linda about the van?'
Wilf took a gulp of wine. 'I did. She said we should tell the police about it, but I think it's a waste of time. What are they going to do?'

Alan nodded. 'Well they didn't do much about Peter or Jodie's break in, I must admit.'

'Exactly,' agreed Wilf, taking another drink from the glass.

Alan asked if the van was still there.
Wilf shook his head. 'No, I've just checked.'

'So, what are you proposing?' asked Alan.
Wilf thought for a moment. 'We've either got to catch him at it or find nicked gear in his van.'
Alan was sceptical. 'That won't be easy mate. He's probably flogging it before he comes back for more.'

'True,' Wilf replied, 'but it's worth a try.'
Alan thought for a moment. 'Ok, I'm up for it, but what do we do if we catch him?'
Wilf smiled. 'I'm sure we can persuade him not to return.'

They finished off the bottle of wine and Wilf wandered back along the jetty to his boat.

Lennie gave his little terrier a final walk along the grass banking by the ranch. Although, the blinds were down, the lights were still on, so he went in.

He was surprised to find two female police officers there. One was a bit frumpy but the other one, not too bad looking. He smiled. She gave a little nod. He always did have a thing about women in uniform. Linda explained what had happened and that they were waiting for the boat to arrive in the marina so they could look inside.

'Might get a few clues,' the frumpy one said. The other officer asked him if he had seen anyone suspicious hanging around.

He laughed. 'Half the people in this marina are suspicious love.'

The frumpy one gave a humourless frown of disapproval. Lennie wasn't sure if it was his frivolity or the use of the term 'love.' He chuckled; she was probably a feminist campaigner.

Vernon and the woman's husband brought the narrowboat alongside the service point. It could remain there overnight then be moved to another mooring in the morning. Vernon had said he would locate a carpenter to repair the front doors.

The two officers were on the boat for about twenty minutes before returning to the building.

'Not much to go on,' said the frumpy one to the couple. 'They made quite a mess though.'

Vernon raised his eyes. 'Why not state the bleeding obvious,' he thought.

Lennie was tempted to ask if she had found any clues but thought better of it.

The officer continued. 'Well that's about it for now, there's not much more we can do. We'll arrange for

SOCO to come tomorrow, so try not to disturb anything.'

She handed them a piece of paper with a crime number on it. 'You'll need this for the insurance people, oh, and one of these.' It was a Victims of Crime Support Services leaflet.

Lennie winked as the officers left the building, and he wasn't looking at the frumpy one.

Vernon saw him. 'You, cheeky sod,' he said.

The dejected couple studied the two pieces of paper. 'Well I hope they find something tomorrow,' said the husband.

Lennie smiled at the woman who was making a fuss of his little dog.

'You never know,' he said. 'Maybe they'll catch somebody.' He was tempted to say, 'don't hold your breath.' But he didn't.

'Do you have a number for a local hotel?' the husband asked Vernon.

Vernon asked why they needed a hotel.

'Well we can't go back on the boat until those fingerprint people have been tomorrow.'

Linda said. 'There's no need to do that, you can eat with us tonight.'

'That's very kind,' replied the woman, 'but we still need to sleep somewhere.'

'What about these sofas in here?' said Vernon. 'They're nice and comfy, and we have a couple of sleeping bags you can use.'

The couple looked at each other and smiled. 'Ok,' said the man, 'thank you very much.'

That night over dinner and a few drinks they expressed how touched they both were by the support and kindness they had received.

CHAPTER ELEVEN

The Dry Dock

Jimmy turned the ignition key and the Beta engine burst into life beneath his feet. It had been three years since the hull had been blacked and today he and Eva were taking Rainbow to a dry dock to have it re-done; he could already feel the pain in his wallet. It was a cold but bright morning, certainly better than the previous week of nonstop rain and howling wind.

'Let go,' he shouted to Eva. She untied the bow line and jumped on board. He pulled the stern line through the mooring ring and coiled it up. Pushing down on the throttle the boat moved gently astern away from the pontoon. It was a tight turn as there was a line of moored boats behind. He pushed the tiller bar hard over, gave it a burst of forward motion and slowly the bow came around in the direction of the marina entrance. Jock, hearing the noise of the engine, had come out onto the stern of his boat, the cold breeze rippling his kilt around his exposed kneecaps.

'Have a good trip,' he shouted.

'Remind Lewis to pick us up tonight,' Jimmy called back.

Jock waved. 'Will do.'

Although it was only to be a short journey it was good to be out on the canal again. A few boats were moored along the towpath, some in a better state of repair than others. Jimmy often wondered how some of them ever got a Boat Safety Certificate. One had a pile of old pallets and a rusting generator sitting beside the towpath and a few empty beer cans were scattered amongst the grass. The roof of the boat was covered with what can only be described as junk. Jimmy shook his head. 'Unbelievable,' he said loudly.

Eva came up on to the stern with two mugs of tea and a packet of digestive biscuits.

'What did you say?' she asked.
He pointed. 'I was moaning about that. Why do they have to make so much bloody mess everywhere?'

'I bet it doesn't have a licence,' she added. Jimmy laughed. 'Course not, yet they seem to get away with it.'

'How long will it take to get there?' she asked.
He checked his watch. 'We should arrive about three all being well. There shouldn't be many boats about this time of year.'

Eva took the tiller bar from him. 'Fishermen up ahead,' she said. Jimmy had a love hate relationship with fishermen, and no doubt they with him.
She slowed the boat as they passed by them. Reluctantly they raised their long poles which nearly reached to the opposite bank. Few made eye contact with the pair. Jimmy could never understand why they all looked so bloody miserable.

As they rounded a short bend Eva had to shield her eyes from the glare of the wintery sun. Jimmy waved as a pair of Lycra-clad joggers ran by. He smiled as he remembered Jodie and Eva's short-lived obsession with running. It had been part of a new year's resolution to keep fit and lose weight. They had even suggested that he and Lewis joined them. That was never going to happen. After a month of being battered by the weather, splattered in mud and chased by dogs, they hung up their new running shoes and joined a Pilates class in town. Much safer, and no, Jimmy and Lewis weren't doing that either.

It was only a short distance now before they reached the first lock. Eva swerved suddenly to avoid a small tree that had fallen from the bank into the canal. The resulting wash engulfed then displaced two moorhens who had been blissfully resting on the waterlogged obstruction. She reduced the speed and glided the boat alongside the bank. Jimmy jumped off with the midline which he tied off around one of the mooring bollards. She handed him the windlass and he walked towards the lock. It was empty. He closed the bottom gates, irritated that the previous boater hadn't done so when leaving. Walking back to the top gates he wound up the paddles. 'If only they were all as easy as this one,' he thought. He sat on the balance beam and watched the water tumbling into the lock chamber from the canal.

Eva had stepped off the stern of the boat and was stroking two inquisitive horses that were peering over the fence at her. It brought back memories of when she used to ride Icelandic ponies on the beach as child. She had spent the first twelve years of her life living in the Netherlands.

Her father was Dutch and her mother an English musician. He worked for a global oil company based in Rotterdam, but they lived in the coastal resort of Bergen aan Zee. Eventually he was re-located to London. Often, she and Jimmy returned to visit her grandparents who still lived in the small village of Oudewater. Both they and Eva had tried to teach Jimmy Dutch, but to no avail.

Jimmy called. He had dropped the paddles and opened one of the gates. Eva gave the horses a final pat, untied the midline and steered the boat into the lock. Jimmy closed the gate behind her. He hooked the midline around a bollard and passed it back to her. She pulled it tight. The water level in the chamber started to drop as he wound up the paddles on one of the bottom gates.

Eva constantly checked the concrete sill behind her. She didn't want the stern of the boat settling on that. As the last of the water seeped out he pushed on the balance beam and opened the gate.

Unhooking the midline, he threw it onto the roof. Eva steered the boat out and Jimmy closed the gate. She placed the stern close to the bank and he jumped onboard.

'I'll make another cuppa,' he said, disappearing below.

'Not too strong,' she called after him.

Jimmy smiled, remembering his tug skipper grandfather who would only drink tea if the spoon would stand up in it. He had made it the same ever since.

Jimmy enjoyed being on the canals, but they were tame compared with the Thames. He missed working on the river, those rapidly moving tides which pour from the sea into that narrow channel twice a day, challenging the best of boatman. After sixteen years of working for the PLA he knew the stretch between the Pool of London and Gravesend like the back of his hand, and he never tired of the contrasts along its bank; the massive buttresses that support the historic and iconic bridges which carry road and rail across the river and the eddies which dance and swirl around their base as the tide ebbs and floods. Old wharfs and docks which once serviced ships from across the world as they offloaded their goods; now turned into expensive houses and offices. Below Limehouse Lock, was the Thames Barrier built in 1974 to prevent London from flooding, and the tall masts of the clipper 'Cutty Sark' as it rests in its dry dock at Greenwich. The alacritous winds which sweep across the marshes on the lower reaches; all of this and more had been in Jimmy's DNA since childhood, and although his job in Bristol harbour was interesting it was no substitute for Old Father Thames.

In the absence of any oncoming craft Eva positioned the boat into the middle of the canal. Beyond the hedgerows, pond sized muddy puddles lay rippling in the waterlogged fields. In one she could see a farmer offloading feed from a trailer to a herd of hungry, expectant cows. Jimmy passed her up a mug of tea, just as she liked it, weak and milky.

'You ok for a minute?' he asked.

She was, it gave her the opportunity to think. She loved Jimmy dearly but he was hyperactive which left little time for contemplation. Apart from the low thud of the engine it was the quiet and stillness of the countryside that always seduced her, though at times she still missed the hustle and bustle of London. After the family had moved back from the Netherlands, they found a house on Blackheath, in South London. Eva enjoyed it there. Greenwich Park with its fantastic views of the Thames was on her doorstep and she spent many happy summer evenings relaxing there with other sixth form students. It was on one such balmy day that her first serious boyfriend introduced her to wacky baccy.

Eva always had a rebellious streak, even as a child. She often smiled when she remembered her mother chasing her around the house with a wooden spoon, rarely catching her.

A sudden shout from the towpath interrupted her pondering. It was a cyclist. She slowed the engine.

'A boat has slipped its moorings just around the bend, it's blocking the canal,' he shouted.

Eva waved. 'Thanks for that.'

Jimmy had heard the exchange and came up onto the stern. Taking the tiller bar from Eva he steered the boat around the short curve. The obstructing craft was wallowing about at the mercy of the breeze. There was no obvious sign of an occupant, so he carefully nudged the bow of Rainbow against the port side of the narrow boat. He had come across this before. No doubt a passing boat going too fast had created an undertow, pulling the mooring pins from the soft bank. Slowly he manoeuvred the boat round until he was alongside it. Eva jumped across and retrieved the bow line from the water, the heavy mooring pin was still attached to the end. Jimmy had just started to push the boat towards the bank when an angry and distorted face appeared at the window.

'What yer doing? Clear off,' he shouted aggressively.

'You're adrift, mate,' Jimmy called back. The doors slowly opened. Wearing what looked like an old army greatcoat, the dishevelled character emerged wide eyed onto the stern. He vaguely scanned the scene before him, clearly confused as to his current predicament.

'You alright dude? Heavy night was it?' asked Jimmy. He wasn't sure if it was drink or drugs, but he was clearly on another planet. The greatcoat scratched his matted hair and muttered something inaudible. Being unsteady on his feet Jimmy was afraid he might fall over the side into the canal.

'Hold tight fella,' he called, as he gave the boat one final nudge into the bank.

Eva jumped ashore with the bowline. Jimmy asked him to pull the stern line out of the water. He was met with a vacant and somewhat disinterested expression. Taking the pole from the roof Jimmy scooped the line up from the water and threw it onto the bank, followed by a club hammer. Eva drove the spikes back into the ground and re-connected the lines.

'There mate, you're secure once again,' said Jimmy.

He nodded. 'You got any smokes?' he mumbled.

Jimmy smiled. 'Not any more mate, I gave up recently, too expensive.'

The greatcoat fumbled in his pocket and produced a half smoked roll up not much bigger than a dog end.

'You got a light?' he asked, shakily placing it between his lips.

Jimmy took a lighter from his pocket and held it to the stub, being careful not to burn his nose.

The greatcoat inhaled, emitted a loud rasping cough, then spat phlegm into the canal.

Jimmy stepped back quickly. 'You need to look after yourself pal.'

They went back on board Rainbow. As Jimmy untied and pushed off Eva waved. There was no response.

'How do people let themselves get like that?' she asked Jimmy.

Jimmy shook his head. 'It's bloody awful, they'll probably find him floating face down in the canal one day, and he won't be the last.'

'The sad thing is,' she said, 'I doubt anyone will miss him.'

It was just after four o'clock in the afternoon and darkness was descending as they arrived at the dry dock. It was housed inside a small marina on the outskirts of a picturesque town. There were several privately owned moored boats, and a small hire fleet. They had worked through seven more locks and three swing bridges. One of the bridges was too heavy for Eva to open and close, so Jimmy had to moor up and help her. Eva was all in, she just wanted to get warm, have a shower and eat. They had the option of staying on board in the dry dock whilst the hull was being blacked, but Jodie and Lewis had invited them to stay on their boat.

Jimmy kept the engine just above tick over as Rainbow crept slowly into the marina towards the jetty on the far side, where they were to moor.

'Isn't that Allison's old boat over there?' asked Eva.

Jimmy glanced across at the line of boats. 'It is,' he replied, 'looks like it could do with a bit of TLC though.'

Eva agreed. 'Shame, it used to look so nice, never could work out why she sold it.'

Jimmy shrugged. 'It's a big boat for one, a narrowboat's more practical for her to handle.'

Luckily Lewis had remembered to pick them up and take them back to Crockenhill Marina. Eva though was dreading the journey, Lewis drove far too fast for her liking, particularly around country lanes.

'Alright guy's?' he said, as they stepped ashore. 'You made it then?'

Eva muttered to herself. 'Obviously, we're here.'

It was as they left the dry dock and turned onto the main road towards town that Lewis asked if they had heard about the boat which was broken into. They hadn't.

'Wilf thinks it's a bloke staying in a white van by the entrance,' he said.

'I've seen that,' replied Jimmy.

'Why does he suspect him?' asked Eva. Suddenly Lewis hit the brake as the car in front slowed. As usual he was too close to the rear end of it. Eva shook her head in disbelief. Lewis continued talking as if nothing had happened.

'No idea,' he replied. 'But it would add up wouldn't it? We always said it couldn't be anyone in the marina nicking things.'

For the remaining miles Eva sat in the back with her eyes closed, thankful for the belt anchoring her firmly to the seat. The conversation between the two men had predictably turned to football which bored her rigid. As they both supported different teams it usually turned into an argument. When they arrived back at the marina Jodie was waiting with a large glass of wine which Eva urgently needed to calm her nerves.

'Has he been driving like a lunatic again?' she asked.

Eva took the glass from her. 'Complete nutter,' she replied. 'Thinks he's a rally driver.'

Jodie laughed. 'He's only driven like it since we left London. I think it's because there's less traffic.'

After dinner Lewis and Jimmy went outside to have a recreational smoke and, no doubt, continue their argument about which was the best football team. The girls, glad for some peace and quiet, settled down on the sofa to watch the television. It wasn't long before the combination of the wine and tiredness took effect and Eva fell fast asleep.

CHAPTER TWELVE

Haunting

Vernon waved as the couple who were burgled on the towpath slipped their mooring lines and moved slowly away from the pontoon. They had, in the end, stayed for a week which afforded them enough time to have their front doors repaired, but they were now keen to resume their journey. Vernon was cradling a particularly good bottle of red wine that they had given him.

'Nice people,' said Bert loudly.
Vernon hadn't heard him approach behind him.

'Christ, I nearly dropped the bottle,' he said.
Bert eyed the wine. 'Hope yer going to share that.'
Vernon chuckled. 'No chance, mate.'
Bert asked if they had heard anymore from the police.

'Not a thing,' replied Vernon, before heading off towards his boat.

It was not long after Bert had joined Jeb and Bruce in the ranch building that the first of the couriers arrived. Jeb observed him keenly as he handed Linda a not very large package which she had to sign for on a small handheld machine. He watched through the window as the long-wheeled base transit exited the marina with no regard for the 10mph speed limit.

'No wonder the high streets are dying,' he snorted. 'All these people buying stuff online. Yesterday, three of those vans delivered parcels here and that's going on all around the country, seven days a week.'

Bert stirred his coffee. 'Mur's one of 'em. She orders stuff then sends it back the next day.'

Jeb shook his head. 'Bloody madness.'

Bruce said, 'I suppose it's useful for people who don't have time to go shopping.'

'Oh please,' replied Jeb, 'the shops are open all weekend. No, it's just laziness.'

Bert took out a tin and rolled one of his pencil thin cigarettes. 'Can't remember when I last bought any clothes,' he said.

The other two chuckled. 'We can see that,' said Bruce.

Bert stood up to go outside and light up. 'You two can snigger. I used to get all my clothes at Carnaby Street when I was a teenager.'

'Blimey, he was a style icon,' laughed Bruce.

'Does your Julia buy anything online?' asked Jeb.

Bruce nodded. 'Occasionally, you don't have much choice these days, the way the high streets are going, and it's often cheaper.'

When Bert came back into the building he was looking slightly perplexed. He sat down at the table.

'I've just been talking to that woman outside,' he said, as if they should know who he meant.

Jeb asked, 'What woman?'

'You know,' he replied, 'the one with the three-legged greyhound. She came into the marina about a month ago.'

Bruce laughed. 'That's a bit of a handicap in a race.'

'What about her?' asked Jeb.

Bert sniffed and shifted his bum on the seat. His piles were playing up. 'She thinks her boat is haunted.'

The other two glanced at each other.

'Haunted by what?' asked Bruce.

'A ghost,' replied Bert tetchily. 'What else would it be?'

Bruce shrugged his shoulders. 'Imagination probably, I don't believe all that nonsense. Once you're dead, you're dead, and why would it haunt a boat?'

'Maybe it lived there before she got it,' said Bert. 'An earthbound spirit that needs to move on. I've read about such things.'

Jeb went to the fridge and returned with a pint of milk, which he almost drank in one go.

'So, what makes her think it's haunted?' he asked Bert.

'Strange noises, 'he replied, 'and always around midnight. Tapping and scraping as if someone's trying to get into the boat.'

'Or out,' said Bruce, laughing.

Bert continued. 'The other night she got up to use the loo and it felt as if someone was watching her.'

Bruce chuckled. 'She should close the curtains then.'

'It's alright for you to be flippant,' said Bert. 'The woman's really worried.'

116

Jeb asked if she was taking any medication.

'How the hell would I know that,' retorted Bert. 'I wasn't going to ask if she was taking tablets for being a nutter. She seems pretty normal to me.'

'Why did she tell you anyway?' asked Bruce. Bert shook his head. 'I don't know, maybe she felt I was approachable.'

Bruce laughed. 'Christ. That would be a first.'

Jeb though for a moment. 'If she's really concerned, get her to have a word with that Glenda, she's into talking with spirits apparently. She's moored over on the Dark Side.'

'Well she would be,' said Bruce chuckling. 'I'll get some more coffee.'

Before the ranch closed Bert asked Linda where the woman he had been talking with was moored in the marina. That evening he and Mur went to her boat to tell her about Glenda, the medium, and how she might be able to help. Walking back Mur asked him if he believed in ghosts.

'It's like UFO's,' he replied. 'You have to keep an open mind.' He stopped and looked up at the sky. 'Look at the vastness of that. Who knows what's really out there?'

He never failed to surprise her.

Inside the boat the woman had a final tidy round, not that it was messy, just lived in.

Glenda, the medium, was coming at eight o'clock. She drew the curtains and waited with some apprehension. The boat rocked slightly as someone

117

stepped into the bow well. It was followed by a soft knock. The three-legged greyhound barked. The woman opened the door.

'Hello, my dear,' said Glenda. 'Let's see if we can sort out your little haunting, shall we?'
She bustled in carrying a heavily patterned cloth bag. She wore a long necklace of coloured beads which she constantly fiddled with when talking.

'Would you like a drink?' asked the woman. Glenda settled into one of the chairs. 'Just a small gin, if you have it. It helps to open the channels you understand.'

'I don't have any alcohol I'm afraid,' replied the woman, 'just tea or coffee.'
Glenda gave a disappointed smile. 'Not to worry then my dear, I'm sure we'll manage without it.' She twiddled her beads with both hands as if massaging them. 'So, this naughty spirit's been bothering you?' she asked.
The woman nodded and sat down beside her. 'Well I wouldn't say naughty,' she said, 'just disturbing.'

Glenda chuckled. 'Not naughty yet maybe, but they can become so.'

She opened the cloth bag and took out a pair of tall candle sticks which she put on the table, then two beeswax candles which she placed in the holders. 'Darker the better,' she said. Next to emerge from the bag was a portable CD player.

'They seem to love classical music,' she explained. 'Especially Beethoven, it seems to draw them in. It's all about the vibrations you see,' she laughed, 'although I did have one who liked Punk music. Some people have no taste.'

She opened the lid and put in a CD. 'Funny thing is it also works on my Boris, seems to settle him down, he gets quite stressed'.

'Is that your partner?' asked the woman. Glenda laughed, 'Oh no dear, he's my pet python.' The woman nodded. 'Oh, right.'

Glenda pulled from her pocket a small coloured glass bottle, the contents of which she proceeded to sprinkle around the table and chairs where they would be sitting. 'Liquid lavender,' she said. 'Just in case.'

'In case of what?' asked the woman nervously.

'Well dear, sometimes they can become a little agitated, particularly if it's a child, or they're having a problem communicating. We don't want any accidents, do we? The lavender will keep us safe.'

The woman was now feeling distinctly uneasy at the requirement for this protection. Glenda lit the candles. 'Now turn off the lights, my dear,' she said.

This produced an eerie glow as the flickering flames cast long finger like shadows onto the walls of the boat.

Glenda took the woman's hand. 'Now dear, let me explain what's going to happen. I will speak with my spirit guide. He's an old American native Indian called Leaning Tree. He will help us make contact with your spirit.'

The woman whispered. 'He's not my spirit.'

Glenda smiled. 'He is now my dear.'

'How do you know it's a he?' The woman asked.

'I don't, but it usually is, women don't tend to dwell, they like to move on,' she replied.

Glenda took a deep breath and closed her eyes. The heavy breathing continued for a few minutes. Then she spoke. 'Leaning Tree, are you there? Please, come through to us Leaning Tree.'

Another deep breath. For a moment nothing, then suddenly her whole body started to twitch as if she was having some kind of fit. Eventually she exhaled deeply and opened her eyes.

'He's here,' she said in a low, almost inaudible voice.

The woman looked around the dark boat half expecting to see a ghostly apparition wearing an Indian headdress and carrying a tomahawk.

'He wants to know if you have lost anyone recently?' asked Glenda.

The woman thought for a moment. 'My cat died in the winter,' she whispered. 'It was very old.'

'No dear,' said Glenda, 'it would have to be in human form.'

Glenda closed her eyes and for a short time seemed to engage in a conversation with her spirit guide. Finally she said, 'Thank you Leaning Tree and God bless.'

'Has he gone?' asked the woman.

'Oh no, dear,' replied Glenda. 'He will act as our gate keeper.' She patted her hand. 'We don't want any unwanted spirits coming through now do we?'

She pressed the button on the CD player and the sounds of Beethoven's Moonlight Sonata filled the cabin. 'They like this one,' she said, drumming her fingers on the table. 'It draws them close to us. Are you there, lost friend?' she called in a loud voice. 'We are here to help you move on. My name is Glenda, what's yours? Tap if you are with us.' The woman shivered, she wanted to put more coal on the stove but dare not move outside the lavender circle.

'Don't worry,' said Glenda, sensing the woman's unease. 'They can be shy sometimes.' She turned up the volume on the CD player.

'Is there anybody there?' she called. 'Tap once for yes, and twice for no.'

Both women sat quietly in the still of the darkened boat. A sliver of light from the half-moon slipped between the drawn curtains, and the water lapped gently against the side of the hull. Suddenly one of the candles flickered wildly before extinguishing altogether. The woman gasped.

'Now we're getting somewhere,' said Glenda. She closed her eyes and took another deep breath. 'Welcome friend,' she said. 'Are you looking for someone on the earth plane?'

Again, the woman shivered. Although there was still a warm glow from the solid fuel stove, the temperature in the boat had dropped dramatically.

121

Glenda continued. 'Do you want to communicate with us? Give us sign.'

Without warning a patterned china fruit bowl that had been sitting in the middle of the table flew off and smashed into pieces on the floor. The woman shrieked. 'Oh, my god!' Glenda took the woman's hand. 'Calm down dear, it's only frustration.' She turned off the CD player.

'Can you tell me your name?' she asked, staring into the gloom, her long fingers fiddling rapidly with the neck beads. She sighed loudly and coughed before turning to the woman.

'Who is Oli?' she asked softly. The woman gasped. For a minute or so she was unable to speak. 'Oli, he was my brother,' she replied tearfully.

'What happened to him? 'asked Glenda.

'He died in a motorcycle crash when he was twenty-five,' she sobbed, 'but that was thirty years ago.'

Glenda smiled. 'That doesn't matter dear. He's the same age now as when he passed.'

She closed her eyes once more. 'Ok Oli. I'll ask her. He's saying do you remember when you fell in the lock and he pulled you out with the boat hook?' The woman smiled as the cobweb of tears wetted her cheeks. 'I was only eight, we used to go on narrowboat holidays with our parents every year. I was running, something I had been told not to do, then my foot caught in a mooring ring and splash.'

Glenda said, 'He wants you to know that he's alright and the reason he came back was to tell you

122

how pleased he is that you are now living on a boat, something you always said you wanted to do.'

'Can you tell him I love and miss him dreadfully?' she asked.

Glenda smiled. 'He knows that and says he misses you too, Abi.'

The woman smiled. 'He was the only one who used to call me that.'

Glenda stared ahead as if seeing beyond the darkness. 'It's time to return now Oli. Leaning Tree is waiting for you. Go towards him.'

The candle on the table suddenly re-ignited and the room warmed. 'He's gone,' Glenda said.

Abi dabbed her eyes. 'That was beautiful,' she said. 'I really can't believe it was him.'

Glenda blew out the candles and put them, the holders and the CD player back into the heavily patterned bag. Abi turned on the lights. She looked at the smashed pieces of the china fruit bowl on the floor and laughed. 'That belonged to my parents, Oliver always hated it.'

'I think I'll have that cup of tea now,' said Glenda, looking tired.

That night Abigail slept soundly. Midnight came and went and nothing disturbed her slumber. In the morning a single red rose lay on the table where the fruit bowl had been. Abigail picked it up and smelt the dark velvety petals. It was the same one that she had placed on Oliver's coffin as he was buried.

When Glenda arrived back at her boat, she took two mice from the freezer and placed them in the microwave to defrost. After giving Boris his dinner she settled down with a large gin and tonic.

Abigail hadn't intended revealing anything to anybody about last night's spiritual experience. Unfortunately, she had underestimated Mur's interrogation skills, honed over many years whilst extracting gossip, often from those trusted with the subject's confidence. The following morning Abigail had taken some washing to the laundry room, a big mistake. This was Mur's lair where she practiced her art. During the next hour the combination of Mur's probing and the hypnotic effect of the rotating drum induced Abigail to reveal every detail of her encounter with 'the other side'.

After Abigail had left, clutching her clean washing, Mur reported back to Bert and Julia and the well-oiled wheel of Chinese whispers cranked into top gear. There was nothing the residents of the marina liked more than a good nonfactual gossip. By the time Mur's initial revelations had spread around the Ranch Sector, it had been so distorted as to suggest that Abigail had experienced a manifestation of supernatural ectoplasm.

During the next few weeks several people beat a path to Glenda's door. Some out of curiosity, others hoping to contact a loved one, or maybe not so loved. Few however replicated Abigail's discarnate experience. Glenda explained that contacting the Elysian Fields is like making an international phone call. If they're not in, it just keeps on ringing. She would laugh and say, 'unfortunately you can't leave a message.' The despondent visitors, used to instant gratification and communication, left Glenda's boat feeling spiritually disenfranchised and sought solace on social media.

CHAPTER THIRTEEN

Words
Words can inspire. And words can destroy.
'Robin Sharma'

Of course, it was not true that a Smart car had to be rescued from a pothole in the track leading to the marina. Nor was it factual that the marina was being sold as a fish farm, or that a person on the Dark Side had contracted the Coronavirus. But when these little droplets of mis information enter the auricle of the recipient, they provide a stimulus to an otherwise uneventful day. Just as a germ needs a vehicle to spread infection so does tittle tattle.

So, it was that Rita, a seasoned carrier, happened to stumble upon a scene which to someone less disposed to erroneous assumption would have been ignored.

The two men had first met at the hospital in Bristol where Luke now worked after he and Ryan had moved down from London to Crockenhill Marina. Luke welcomed his newfound friendship with Haseeb, a radiologist, particularly as there was normally very little time to socialise in a busy hospital environment.

Often after work they would go for a drink to the Drunken Surgeon, a pub just around the corner from the hospital. It was lively and noisy, mainly down to the many student doctors and nurses who frequented the place. It was during one of these evenings that Haseeb seemed unsettled and distracted, unlike his normal attentive and easy going self. Luke asked if he was alright.

He half smiled. 'Just a lot on my mind now, but thanks for asking.'

Luke said he was always there if he ever wanted to talk.

Haseeb took his hand and held it. 'I know, you are a good friend.'

It was halfway through the following week, when not having seen him, Luke enquired at the Radiology Department as to his whereabouts. They said he had taken a few days off, domestic issues apparently. Although Luke had his mobile number he was reluctant to intrude, after all he had not known him that long. The following morning though Haseeb messaged him. 'U up 4 a drink @ Surgeon 2 nite.' Luke was relieved to hear from him and texted back. 'Ok wot time?'

The reply was swift, 'The usual.'

When Luke arrived at the crowded pub, he was shocked at Haseeb's appearance. His face was drawn with pronounced bags under his bloodshot eyes. Recognising Luke's concern, he gave a little laugh.

'I haven't been sleeping too well lately.'

'What on earth has happened?' asked Luke. For a moment he was unsure if Haseeb had heard, it was as if part of him was absent. Then in a barely audible voice he said, 'Six years we were together, now it's over.' A tear started running down his strained face.

'Just like that,' he said, clicking his fingers. Luke reached across the table and took both his hands in his. 'Is this your partner we're talking about.'

Haseeb nodded.

'Well what did she say? asked Luke. 'There must be a reason.'

Haseeb took out a tissue and dabbed his eyes. He smiled. 'It wasn't a she.'

Luke's heart missed a beat. Haseeb shrugged and shook his head. 'Another man, younger apparently. But why after all this time? I thought we were......'

Again, he started to cry, a low pitiful sob. Luke moved across to where he was sitting and put a comforting arm around his shoulder. Haseeb laid his head on Luke's chest. He could smell the cologne that Haseeb had hurriedly splashed on before leaving home. It was 'Montblanc Légende'. The same one as Ryan wore. 'Funny thing,' he thought. They had never discussed partners, or the lack of them. Maybe even in the 21st century there was still a sub conscious-assumption that people had a 'normal' relationship, whatever that meant.

Haseeb sat up and again wiped his eyes. 'Oh, I'm sorry Luke, I didn't mean to..............'

Luke interrupted. 'Don't worry, I understand, believe me.'

Haseeb gave him a quizzical look. 'You do?'

Luke nodded. 'I do, yes.' Their eyes met and for a moment no words were spoken.

Haseeb picked up the empty glasses from the table. 'I'll get some more drinks.'

'Just a soft one for me,' called Luke. 'Don't forget I'm driving.'

Luke took out his mobile phone and rang Ryan to let him know that he would be home late. Ryan was used to it as meetings at the hospital often overran.

It was close to nine o'clock when they eventually left the pub. They pushed their way past a group of students huddled together outside the doorway. Luke could never understand why student doctors and nurses smoked. Haseeb had drunk two more large glasses of red wine and they were taking effect.

'Are you going to be alright getting home?' asked Luke.

'I'm fine,' replied Haseeb, giving Luke a long hug. 'My flat isn't far from here.'

Luke could still smell the 'Montblanc Légende'. It was fading, but still sensual.

'Thanks for being a good listener,' said Haseeb, before walking off. He stopped on the corner to wave. Luke waved back then walked slowly back to his car in the hospital car park.

'What do you mean, you're going to the doctors again?' shouted Bob, Rita's long-suffering ex-husband. They still spoke on the phone, but only when she rang him.

'I'm losing weight,' she replied.

'Course you are,' he retorted, 'you don't eat anything. If you ate as much as you smoked you wouldn't have a problem.'

She didn't get any sympathy from him, but then she knew that when she rang. She disconnected the call on her mobile. From the window of her boat, which was moored on the Dark Side of the marina, she could see someone's plastic hose reel bobbing about in the ruffled water, a casualty of the recent Storm Dennis. Rita had few friends in the marina or elsewhere, which just fuelled her frustration at the cards she felt she had been dealt.

Her doctor, a kindly man nearing retirement, nodded sympathetically as she listed the ailments that had once again brought her to his door. Chief amongst these was her supposed weight loss. After examining her, and to be on the safe side, he agreed to send her for a scan at the General Hospital. When he asked about the smoking she said she was cutting down. He smiled. 'Good.'

Two weeks later she received an email from Linda informing her that there was an NHS letter in the ranch building for her to collect. It was the date of her hospital appointment.

Vernon, who was re-stocking the freezer with ready meals, watched as she opened it.

'What's up Rita?' he shouted. 'You've got a face liked a smacked arse.'

She ignored him and left. Subtleness was never Vernon's strong point.

Rita's was the last appointment of the day. Due to the rush hour the journey from Crockenhill Marina to the hospital had taken her longer than expected. The hospital car park was as usual full. She drove around for several minutes looking for a space. There was none. Frustrated she drove out onto Chalmont Road. A short way along at the corner of a junction stood a pub. As she drove past a Range Rover was pulling out of a parking space, so she quickly pulled in. Opening the door and stepping out she checked the sign attached to the lamppost. 'Max two hours.'

'Perfect,' she thought.

Walking back along the pavement towards the hospital she glanced up at the sign outside the pub. It was swinging gently between two rusted wrought iron supports. There was a faded picture of an elderly man in a frockcoat with his spectacles resting on the end of a bulbous red nose. It was called the Drunken Surgeon.

Two months had passed since Haseeb's partner of six years had suddenly walked out on him. During that time the relationship between him and Luke had become more intimate as their fondness for each other grew. Occasionally they would retreat to Haseeb's flat for a meal and some quiet time alone. Of course, Luke was troubled that he had been lying to Ryan. But where was the harm? It was only a bit of fun, and it wasn't as if he and Haseeb were sleeping together.

Haseeb had left work early and was already in the pub when Luke arrived for their regular evening drink. They embraced. Haseeb kissed him on both cheeks, then sat down and took a large mouthful of Shiraz, his favourite red wine. 'I have something to tell you,' he said taking Luke's hand.

'I'm moving back to Manchester; I've already given in my resignation.'

'But why?' asked Luke, shocked by the suddenness of the decision.

Haseeb sighed deeply. 'I just need to make a fresh start and I can't afford the rent on the flat on my own.'

Luke looked into Haseeb's sad eyes. 'Does it still really hurt that much?'

Haseeb nodded and a small tear appeared in the corner of his eye. 'It's gut wrenching. He was my world and I hate living on my own.'

Luke took a sip of wine from his glass. 'Was it....? Was I......?

Haseeb interrupted him. 'Oh, my dear Luke, without you I couldn't have got this far and who knows, in different circumstances.....' He paused. 'But you have Ryan, and I have to cast my net into a different sea once more.'

'But why Manchester?' asked Luke.

'It's where I came from,' he replied. 'I have lots of friends there, though sadly I don't see my parents anymore.'

Luke asked why not.

He shook his head. 'They never could come to terms with my sexuality.'

'That's terrible,' replied Luke.

Haseeb shrugged. 'It's a cultural thing.'

The pub was getting busy and the noise level increasing. 'Time to go I think,' said Haseeb. Luke agreed. They finished their drinks and went outside. The smokers were still huddled around the doorway. Luke caught a distinct whiff of something illegal. They stood for some time just looking at each other, neither sure of what to say.

Haseeb put his arms around Luke and pulled him close. Then on the pavement without a care, and under the gaze of the Drunken Surgeon, they kissed; it was a long, passionate, parting kiss. The Drunken Surgeon was not the only one witnessing this sad snapshot in time.

After her scan Rita had visited the hospital café on the ground floor. She was parched and needed a cup of tea. There was after all no hurry to return home to the marina and an empty boat. A young woman came from behind the counter and started to clear and wipe the tables. 'Closing up now,' she announced in broken English. Rita smiled and finished her tea. A blast of cold air hit her as she exited the revolving door. She shivered. It was nearly dark and a light rain brushed her cheek. She took a packet of cigarettes from her pocket, lit one and inhaled deeply. It felt good. There was a sign saying, 'No smoking anywhere in the hospital grounds.'

'Why not?' she thought. 'Stuff 'em.'

Crossing the road, she walked back to where her car was parked. Rita wasn't a particularly observant person and it was only the noise from a group of boisterous students outside the pub that made her look up. At first she didn't see the couple locked in an embrace, but as the students dispersed back into the pub it became clear who she was looking at. There was a bus shelter, vandalised and tagged. She ducked inside and watched through the cracked glass.

Luke ran his hand through Haseeb's black hair then stepped back from him. A few words were spoken then Luke walked off towards the hospital car park. Haseeb stood for a moment watching him go, then turned and went home in the opposite direction.

Rita smiled. 'Well who would have thought it?' If she had been a dog her tail would have been wagging at the thought of the succulent bone she was about to chew on. After the two men had disappeared, she skulked back to her car and headed off to the marina.

Alan was sitting on the bow of his boat enjoying his first coffee of the day. The band practice the previous evening had descended into chaos, so they had resorted to stimulating their creative vacuum with a bottle of malt whisky. Jock, who was moored next to Alan, was not normally an early riser. Emerging blurry eyed he put his parrot Nigel's cage onto the roof of his boat, then stood violently scratching his testicles. Nigel, irritated at being woken so early, repeatedly told him to 'fuff off.' Alan laughed. 'Did the midges get you last night mate?'

'They bloody did, and don't ask where, I've 'ardly slept all night.'

'You need to wear some pants underneath that kilt,' Alan said, still amused at his discomfort. Jock chuckled. 'I like to hang free.'

'Anyway, why are you up so early?' asked Alan.

'Didn't you hear that bloody noise at six o'clock this morning?'

Unsurprisingly Alan had not. 'What noise?' he asked.

Spliff, Jock's adopted kitten, came out onto the deck for a fuss. He scooped him up and stroked him.

'Some arsehole was filling an empty coal skuttle, dropping one bloody piece in at a time.'

'Who was it?' asked Alan.

Jock shook his head. 'No idea mate. Bloody naabs,' he exclaimed, in a mock west country accent. Jock had adopted this neologism since arriving at Crockenhill Marina from London. Now he directed it at anyone he considered to be an idiot or fool and, as far as he was concerned, there were plenty of those about.

They heard a door close then Ryan came running along the pontoon. 'Can't stop to chat guys, I'll miss my bus.'

'Don't I get a morning kiss?' called Jock, reverting to his Glaswegian tongue. But Ryan had gone. Alan laughed. 'You want to be careful what you wish for, especially wearing that kilt.'

135

Ryan had secured a job in town at the local library. He had always loved books and enjoyed meeting people, so it was perfect for him. Rita was not a reader, preferring instead to gorge herself on a diet of tacky reality programmes and soaps. It was therefore with some surprise that when returning some books to the shelves, Ryan saw Rita enter the library. She stopped, looked around then headed straight for him. There was no escape. Ryan replaced the books onto the trolly.

'I didn't know you used the library,' he said. She smiled. 'Well, I don't usually dear, but I was passing and thought I'd pop in for a chat.'

Luke knew something was wrong the moment he stepped into the boat that evening. Ryan was not a demonstrative person, but his demeanour and reluctance to engage spoke volumes about the hurt and betrayal he felt. When he did speak, it was to utter just three words.

'How could you?'

There was little point in Luke asking what he was referring to. But how did he know?

Nothing he could say or do would justify his actions. He sat next to Ryan on the sofa, half hoping that he would hit him, at least that would make him feel better. So as the storm waves crashed upon their shores, all Luke could do was wait and hope that the sun would shine again one day.

The following morning Rita had no such concerns. She sat in her dressing gown on the bow of the boat, drinking tea and inhaling her first fag of the day. After dressing and spending a long time studying her slight reflection in the mirror, she drank more tea, ate a slice of toast then went outside. Beyond the fields opposite, the traffic was starting to build up on the road into town.

A voice from behind startled her.

'Morning, love.' Terry was walking Shadow on the narrow strip of grass between the track and the pontoons.

'You left the car window open last night,' he called, pointing. 'Just as well it didn't rain.' Shadow sniffed round her legs, sensing her nervousness. Terry laughed. 'E's alright, 'e's already had his breakfast.' He chuckled to himself. 'Not that you'd make much of a meal.'

She thanked him, unlocked the car, got in and put the window up.

Needing another electricity card she stopped at the ranch building on the way out of the marina. Inside a few people were having a coffee and discussing the results of Saturday's quiz night, so she joined them on the sofa.

'Alright Rita?' asked Peter. 'What's new?'

She yearned to tell them of her discovery the previous evening but knew that doing so would soon get back to Luke. There was always the possibility that Ryan would reveal the informer, but she doubted it. After all, as she saw it, she was doing a service in telling him of Luke's indiscretion. Vernon, who had just finished selling somebody a bag of coal, shouted to her from behind the counter.

'You look 'appier today Rita, like a cat who's got the cream.'

She smiled and drank her coffee.

CHAPTER FOURTEEN

Before the Trains Came

The wooden floorboards had creaked as Linda walked amongst the well-stocked shelves. Felton's was the only independent book shop left in the town. The founding Mr Felton was long gone, and it now fell to his grandson to provide this literary emporium to an ever-decreasing clientele. She could have shopped at one of the large booksellers in the High Street but preferred, where possible, to support the smaller shops. The children's section was not large, squashed in a corner between World Religions and Military History.

She was several minutes into perusing the spines when a soft voice came from behind her.

'May I help you Madam?' Linda turned around. The current Mr Felton, now himself in middle age, wore an open necked blue shirt with bright red braces and sandy coloured trousers.

'Are you looking for anything particular?' he asked.

Linda replied that she was, explaining that her grandson was coming to stay, and he loved anything to do with the canals. He asked how old he was. She said he was nine.

'Lovely age,' he replied. 'Mine are teenagers now, absolute nightmare.'

'Will they take over the shop one day?' asked Linda.

He laughed. 'No chance, they're not interested in this business. I fear I'll be the last.'

'That'll be a shame,' replied Linda.

Moving closer to the shelves he ran his long fingers across the spines. It reminded Linda of a pianist.

'We don't really have much on the canals for children, but there is one here that may be of interest if I can.......... Ah! Here it is,' he said, extracting it from between the other books. He handed it to Linda. 'Wonderful cover, don't you think?' he exclaimed. 'Such colours,' he chuckled. 'As they say in the business, it's the cover that sells the book. I don't recognise the author, but the title indicates that it's all about the decline of the waterways in the twentieth century. It's called, 'Before the Trains Came.'

Linda flicked through the pages. It told the story of one boatman, William Hams, and his family, around the period 1860. There were also some detailed illustrations inside depicting life on the canals during that time.

'I think this will be perfect for him,' said Linda. 'Thank you for your help.'

At the counter she paid, and he wrapped the book for her.

'I hope he enjoys it,' he said, opening the door for her.

'I'm sure he will,' she replied, 'hope to see you again.'

Bert snorted loudly then threw the newspaper he had been reading on the table.

'You couldn't make it up,' he shouted. 'Now they're saying the Wombles were sexist.'

The three wise men were as usual meeting in the ranch building for their morning coffee. Bert was already in a foul mood having succumbed to Mur's nagging about the temperature of the central heating in the boat. 'Put 'er in the Sahara Desert and she'd still feel the bloody cold,' he complained.

'Who says they're sexist?' asked Bruce.

'Some nutter producer in Hollywood,' replied Bert. 'Seems they're making a new television programme about them.'

Bruce picked up the paper and scanned the article. He laughed. 'Apparently the new characters will be 'Gender Neutral' and of different races.'

Bert shook his head. 'What is it with this gender fluid and non-binary stuff? As I see it, if you've got balls, you're a man and if not you're a woman, simple.'

'I don't think it's as straightforward as that these days Bert,' said Jeb.

Again, Bert snorted loudly. 'Then it bloody well should be, it's been like that since Adam and Eve.'

He was just about to continue his expletive laden tirade into political correctness when a young boy came in holding a book.

'This is my grandson, Charlie,' said Linda. The three men said hello to him. 'How old are you then Charlie?' asked Bruce.

He replied he was nine.

Linda laughed. 'Nine, going on sixteen.'

'What book have you got there Charlie?' asked Jeb.

Charlie sat next to Jeb on the sofa and showed it to him. 'Gran got it for me. It's all about the people who worked the cargo boats on the canal years ago. Did you know they used to be pulled by horses?'

Jeb smiled. 'I did.'

'I would like to have been a kid on one of those boats,' said Charlie.

Bert said that it was a hard life.

'Yeah, but they didn't have to go to school. That would be cool.'

Linda sighed. 'They're the latest words, everything's cool or awesome. As I said, going on sixteen.'

Charlie enjoyed staying with Linda and Vernon on their narrowboat which was moored alongside the ranch building. It was certainly more exciting than the second floor flat in Southampton where he lived with his mum. He especially liked being on board when the wind rocked the boat from side to side and the rain beat on the roof. Vernon also told him silly jokes that made him laugh. Linda had made him a bed up at the stern and after drinking a mug of hot chocolate he lay looking at his new book. He was tired but determined to read the first chapter.

On the front page was a picture of a laden working boat called, Speculator. It was attached by rope to a chestnut coloured horse which was pulling it along the canal on the towing path.

A small woman wearing a long colourful lace bonnet and white apron was walking beside it. The boatman steering at the stern wore a flat cap and a black waistcoat, around his neck a red scarf. Tucked inside his thick leather belt was a windlass for opening the paddles. Beyond the hedgerow, on the opposite side of the canal, men in smocks were cutting hay with a long scythe then pitching it into a cart.

He started to read the first sentence.
'Imagine, young boys and girls just like you used to work on the canals with their parents. Their boats carried cargo all over the country.'
He yawned and blinked his eyes to keep them open.
'There was a small cabin at the stern of the boat where the family all lived. It was a hard...................'

Linda carefully lifted the book from his hands, pulled the duvet up and turned off the light.

'He's fast asleep,' she said to Vernon, who was nodding off himself. It wasn't much later before they retired to bed. It had been a busy day in the ranch building with lots of people wanting coal, fuel and gas. Soon the boat was in darkness.

Charlie woke with a start. '*Come on Charlie, up you get, William will be wanting you shortly.*'
He sat up in the small bunk bed and rubbed his eyes. Throwing back the coarse brown blankets he jumped down. Ma Hams, wearing a long, thick, red dress, white apron and bonnet was putting more wood onto the stove. He quickly pulled off his nightshirt and got dressed. As he finished putting

on his black leather boots Ma Hams passed him a tin mug filled with strong tea and two thick slices of bread and jam. *'Get that down yer, lad. It's going to be a long day.'*

He looked around the small cosy cabin with its polished brass, lace plates and Roses and Castles painted on the woodwork. There was a shout from outside. *'Come on Charlie, get a move on!'*

He finished the tea and made for the door. *'Don't forget those,'* called Ma, throwing him his flat cap and scarf. Charlie shivered, dawn had just broken, and an eerie mist clung to the canal. William Hams was waiting for him on the towpath, he was a big man with a thick moustache. His clay pipe was clenched firmly between his teeth. He took a pocket watch from his waistcoat pocket, swung it on the silver chain then flicked it open. *'We need to get going shortly if we're to make our destination tonight.'* He turned and walked towards the stable. *'Come on lad, let's get Thunder harnessed up.'*

Charlie looked around him, there we four other boats moored alongside the wharf. Two of them were loaded, sitting heavy in the water and ready to leave. Others were empty awaiting their cargo. Alongside the stable was a tall brick warehouse where goods, both incoming and outgoing, would be stored. A hand operated crane with a long jib stood ready at the water's edge.

Two portly, ruddy faced women dressed like Ma Hams were washing clothes in a huge iron pot which stood over a bed of hot embers. One had a thick wooden stick which she used to stir the garments round and round. The other, using a pair of long wooden tongs, lifted the steaming hot items from the pot, fed them though an old iron mangle, folded them and dropped them neatly into a wicker basket.

The woman with the stick waved it furiously at two young boys who kicked a ball too near the fire. *'Luk ater dat bladder Dig,'* she called angrily. They ran off in fear of a thick ear, or worse.

Thunder was tethered alongside five other horses. *'Come on Thunder lad, time to do some work,'* said William, patting his neck. *'Untie him Charlie and we'll get him harnessed up.'* William picked up the 'Gears' and arranged them onto Thunder's neck and back. He wasn't concerned as he was munching his way through a large bag of oats and chopped hay that Charlie had given him for breakfast. Before leaving the stable William lifted each of Thunder's legs to check that none of his iron horseshoes were wearing out.

Outside, Ma Hams had put two more tin mugs of steaming tea on the roof of the cabin.

'Shall I do horse today?' she asked.

'If yer like love, I'll steer,' called William. She took the bag of feed from around Thunder's neck and hung it on the side of the boat.

'Right Charlie, sort out the towrope and we'll connect him up,' called William.

Charlie went to the bow end of the boat. Next to the towing mast was coiled ninety feet of thick rope. One end had a simple sliced loop hooked over the luby, an iron peg on the side of the mast. He took the other end to William who attached it to Thunder's harness.

'Right I think we're ready to go,' said William.

Ma waved goodbye to some of the other women then walked Thunder forward, stopping only when the rope had uncoiled behind him. William stepped on to the stern of the boat and connected the wooden tiller bar.

'Let go Charlie,' he shouted. Charlie undid the bow line from the mooring ring, coiled it up and laid it on the boat, then ran to the stern and did the same. William held a match to his pipe then signalled to Ma.

'Get on with 'yer,' she called, smacking Thunder's rump.

Suddenly there was a jolt as his hooves bit into the hard ground, slowly the boat with its twenty-five tons of ash and oak planking moved away from the mooring. Once more William checked his pocket watch. *'Not bad lad, we should be there by dark.'*

It took them some time to pass through the ever-burgeoning outskirts of the town with its drab and grimy buildings which seemed to merge into one another. The occasional dead dog or cat floated by along with other rubbish that had found its way into the canal. At the rear of a glue factory a yellow coloured liquid flowed from a steel pipe into the water.

'You steer while I light my pipe,' said William. Charlie smiled; it was always going out. Taking a small leather pouch from his pocket William took a pinch of tobacco, pushed it into the bowl of his pipe

146

then lit it. *'We'll be in the countryside soon, then we can all breathe,'* he said, exhaling a cloud of fruity smelling smoke. Charlie pushed hard on the tiller as they went around a sharp bend. Up ahead Thunder effortlessly plodded on conveying them silently along the waterway.

William called to Ma. *'You ok Love?'* She raised her hand to signal she was.

He laughed. *'Good woman our Ma. She'd walk for miles with Thunder.'*

Vernon cursed, he knew that last can of beer was a mistake, now he urgently needed to pee. Linda had been constantly nagging him to go to the doctors to have a prostate check, but he never listened. He pushed back the duvet, careful not to wake Linda or Charlie. The clock on the shelf showed it was the early hours of the morning. Quietly he walked through the darkened boat to the toilet, or heads. Once inside he closed the door and switched on the light. As he turned, his arm caught the small china mug which sat on a shelf and held the toothbrushes. He tried catching it, but it fell onto the tiled floor, smashing into pieces. He swore under his breath. Linda and Charlie stirred but did not seem to wake.

The noise had in fact jolted Charlie in his sleep. He heard a whooshing noise and he lost sight of the scene before him. Confused he shook his head in the blackness. Then in what was seconds, he was back on the boat and the sun was shining. Beyond the bridge hole he could see the canal as it meandered between thick hedgerows.

147

'*You ok Charlie?*' asked William.
He nodded and blinked. '*I think so.*'

'*Good, we've got a lock coming up after this bend.*'

He took the 'smacking whip' from its hook and gave it three loud cracks, in case another boat was leaving the lock chamber and coming towards them. Ma continued to walk on with Thunder until she got close to the lock then, pulling on his harness, he stopped. William took the tiller bar from Charlie and steered the boat alongside. When he was level with the strapping post, he threw the strap over it then quickly took the boat's line and put two turns around the post, bringing the boat to a gradual halt. William pulled out the windlass that was tucked inside his leather belt and handed it to Charlie. Charlie jumped off and ran up to the lock. The chamber was empty. He pushed on the balance beam to open the gate. Ma looked proudly across at him and smiled. William waved. Then he heard a familiar voice.

'Morning sleepy bones. Good dreams?' It was Linda.

CHAPTER FIFTEEN

The Toll House

They had been monitoring the activities of the white van man for some weeks. Although it had been parked in the same place outside the marina on several occasions, there was still nothing to implicate the driver in any of the recent thefts from boats, Alan, Wilf and Lennie though were convinced of a connection and were determined to prove it.

Wilf left his boat and walked towards the marina entrance. A short way along the track was a boat hire company, one of several that now saturated this popular narrow canal. Alongside an enclosed rubbish point was a car park where hirers could leave their vehicles for the duration of their cruise. Climbing over the rickety style into the field he noticed that the electric fence had been activated as a flock of sheep were now grazing the long course grass. At the far end he pushed open the wooden gate that led to the towpath, it was only a short walk up the hill to the house where the forty-foot trip boat was moored. The very persuasive local waterways charity who operated the boat, had asked Wilf to quote for servicing the engine before the summer season started. He was busy enough already and didn't really want the job but felt obliged to have a look at it.

The red bricked house with its tall chimneys and attractive, colourful hanging baskets stood where it had for over one hundred and fifty years. Beyond its white-fenced front garden was the first of a flight of wide locks that fell down the hill to the canal and fields below. Beside the wooden front porch was a small room with a sliding glass window where, in days gone by, the cargo carrying boatmen would pay a fee to the lock keeper before entering the flight.

Ken Stubbs, now in his late fifties, was the fourth generation of lock keepers to occupy the house with his wife Maggie and two golden retrievers. Their three children had flown the nest, the youngest only recently to Lancaster University. Ken was responsible for the maintenance and upkeep of the flight and its water levels. In recent years a team of volunteers had been recruited to help him achieve this and assist the public. Whilst he welcomed their support, it was no substitution for full time staff, many of whom had been made redundant or not replaced after retirement.

When he did have a day off, he indulged his passion of growing vegetables and flowers in the large garden at the back of the house, a skill he inherited from his father and grandfather. These would be sold to the public in the spring and summer, alongside the fresh eggs from his ducks and hens. His other passion was his two 1960's ex-racing motorcycles, a 500cc Manx Norton and 350 AJS. Both had been painstakingly renovated and were now worth a considerable amount of money.

Ken kept them safely locked in his garage at the side of the house. He had always loved motorcycles and had ridden one since a teenager. Unfortunately, this activity ended five years ago when he was T-boned by a car, resulting in serious injuries and a lengthy stay in hospital. After that Maggie gave him an ultimatum, either the bikes went, or she did. There was really no competition, though he often joked that, 'it was a difficult choice.'

In the front garden, round tables with patterned covers were set out on the neatly cut lawn. Maggie was famous for her cream teas with home-made jam and scones. People came from miles around to enjoy them and watch boats going through the locks. Only being a short distance away the residents of Crockenhill Marina were also regular customers of hers. Maggie was of Irish stock and boaters passing through the flight on St Patrick's day were guaranteed of a glass of whisky.

The twelve seater trip boat was moored alongside a small wooden jetty just above the top lock. Wilf checked the time on his phone it was half past one. He had arranged to meet one of their people at two o'clock, so he had time to spare. The front door of the house was ajar, he opened the gate and went into the garden. The dogs had heard him before he reached the step, they bounded out barking and wagging their tales. They weren't the greatest guard dogs. 'Only me, you silly dogs,' he shouted stroking them.

Maggie called from the kitchen. 'Come in Wilf, kettle's on.'

'That smells good,' he said, sitting down at a long table.

Maggie nodded. 'Homemade bread,' she said. 'I can't be doing with all that supermarket stuff. Now what'll it be, tea or coffee?' He opted for coffee.

She banged on the window to attract the attention of Ken who was digging up one of his plots in the back garden. Thank the Lord that rain stopped. He's been like a fecking bear with a sore head, not being able to get out outside.'

Ken opened the back door, took off his wellington boots and banged them on the wall. 'Earth's still pretty clingy,' he said, 'but it's drying out nicely.' He sat down opposite Wilf. Maggie put three mugs of coffee and some biscuits on the table, then gave the dogs a chew each.

'So, what brings you up here?' he asked Wilf. He told him about the engine needing a service on the trip boat.

Ken nodded. 'It needs it, been chucking out a lot of smoke lately.'

Maggie added, 'It's a grand little project, brings us lots of trade in the summer.'

'I'm surprised you've got time to do it,' said Ken.

Wilf shook his head. 'I haven't really, but it's difficult to say no.'

'So, what's happening at the marina now?' asked Maggie. 'Anything new?'

He shrugged. 'Not really, same old, same old.' Which was an understatement, but he couldn't be bothered going into detail. 'What about you?' he asked.

Ken laughed. 'We're going through yet another re-organisation which will, no doubt, lead to more bloody redundancies and bureaucracy.'

'Are you safe here?' asked Wilf.

He shrugged. 'Who knows? They've been talking about selling these places off for years.'

Wilf asked what they would do if that happened.

Ken shook his head. 'No idea mate, we wouldn't get a mortgage at our time of life.'

Maggie laughed. 'We might have to come and live on a boat in the marina.'

'You could do worse,' said Wilf, finishing his coffee.

'Could you imagine him without his garden?' said Maggie. 'He'd drive me round the fecking bend.'

Wilf checked the time on his phone. 'I'd better get going, he'll be waiting outside.'

'Who's meeting you?' asked Ken, following him out.

'Their Chairman apparently,' replied Wilf.

Ken chuckled. 'Oh yeah, he's alright, bit of a damp rag.'

They stopped by the front gate. 'Any more news on your white van man?' Ken asked.

Wilf shook his head. 'Nothing. He still comes and goes though.'

'Maybe the thefts were nothing to do with him in the first place,' said Ken.

'You might be right,' answered Wilf, who had recently started to have doubts himself.

Throughout breakfast the next morning Charlie tried to convince Linda and Vernon that he really had been there with William and Ma Hams, despite being told it was just a dream.

It was their time off. Alex, the warden, would be manning the ranch building for the next two days along with his dog Tazz. Vernon took a bite from a piece of toast and jam. He never ate much. Charlie did, and was working his way through his second bowl of coco pops.

'So, Charlie,' said Vernon suddenly. 'You reckon that you've steered a seventy-foot loaded working boat?'

Charlie nodded. 'Yeah, but I had William next to me.'

Vernon took a mouthful of tea from his mug. 'Right, we're going down the pub for lunch and taking the boat, so, you can steer it.'

The pub in question was the Three-Legged Mare. It was set back from the canal, about two miles from the marina. Owned by a local brewery it had a large garden, with a small campsite at the back. Having hardstanding canal side moorings, it was popular with boaters as an overnight stop, or to fill up with water and dispose of rubbish. Subsequently in the summer you would be lucky to get alongside, particularly with the amount of hire boats passing through. Charlie looked at Linda for reassurance. She winked at him and nodded.

'Alright then,' he replied, spooning in another mouthful of cereal, 'but don't forget that boat was towed by a horse.'

Vernon laughed. 'Well, we don't 'ave a horse so you'll have to make do with an engine.'

The morning was taken up with shopping in town, something Vernon hated intensely. In the supermarket Charlie trailed behind them, occasionally stopping to look at something, then losing them both between the aisles. Before returning home to the marina they had a coffee in the supermarket café.

Whilst queueing Vernon became impatient with an indecisive couple in front of them.

'You'd think they were buying a bloody house, instead of a sandwich,' he whispered to Linda. She was used to it and ignored him. Charlie was happy though, he was going to gorge himself on a jam donut and strawberry milkshake.

As they were leaving the shop Bruce and Julia from the marina were coming in.

'How's that canal book going Charlie?' asked Bruce.

Charlie wiped some jam from his chin. 'It's really good,' he replied. 'I've been there with 'em.'

Bruce was just about to ask where and with whom when Linda stopped him. 'Don't go there, we'll be here all day.' As Vernon and Linda went through the exit doors into the carpark, Charlie hung back and whispered to Bruce, 'They don't believe me.'

'Come on you,' called Linda.

'What was that all about?' asked Julia.

155

Bruce shook his head and smiled. 'I've no idea.'

Vernon wanted to be away from the marina by half past twelve. Whilst Linda went into the ranch building to see Alex, he and Charlie made the boat ready for departure. Jeb, whose boat was moored at the front of the ranch building, had come out onto the pontoon. 'I hear you're steering today,' he called.

Charlie waved and nodded. 'I am.'

'Well you can't do any worse than him,' he laughed, pointing at Vernon.

Vernon was unplugging the electricity cable and didn't hear him, otherwise a fruity reply would no doubt have been forthcoming. 'Untie the bow line,' he called to Charlie.

'You weren't going without me, were you?' asked Linda, returning from the building.

Vernon laughed as he started the engine. 'It was Charlie's idea, he said you could walk.'

'No, it wasn't,' retorted Charlie. 'You said she's probably gassing to somcone.'

Linda raised her eyebrows. 'That's more like it.' She undid the stern line and coiled it up on the deck.

'Right young Charlie, all yours,' said Vernon handing him the tiller bar. Vernon pushed the throttle down and the boat slid away from the mooring. Charlie kept the tiller bar straight as they passed the bow ends of all the boats moored in the Ranch Sector. Mur, who was hanging washing on a rotary line, waved as they passed her boat. The two swans were swimming close to the small island. Linda hoped they were going to nest there this year, rather than next to a pontoon. She did not want a repeat of last time when Ronnie was chasing and attacking anybody who got too near to the nest.

Approaching the marina entrance Vernon watched to see if Charlie lined the boat up to go through. He did, bringing the bow round into the narrow passage. There was a sudden shout as they drew level with the grass at the canal side sector. Alan and Jock were both holding up cans of beer.

'Well done Charlie,' called Alan. 'You'll be a boatman yet.'

Passing under the lift bridge Vernon slowed the engine ready for the tight turn to port. 'Right, hard over,' he said. Charlie pushed on the tiller bar. 'Good lad,' said Vernon as the boat brushed the opposite bank. 'That's a tight turn.' As the boat straightened Vernon increased the speed.

'This is faster than we used to go with Thunder pulling us,' said Charlie.

Linda smiled. 'That was quieter though, I bet.'

Charlie nodded. 'It was.'

Vernon slowed the engine as they approached a line of moored boats. Linda remarked on the number of them. Vernon said it was due to the lock being closed for repairs further down.

'I hope we can get a mooring outside the pub,' she replied.

On the bow of one boat a man sat mesmerised as a small orange float bobbed about in the water.

'Caught anything?' called Charlie.

The man laughed. 'Only a cold, son.'

157

Vernon shook his head. 'I can't think of anything more boring than fishing, I just don't get it.'
Linda whispered to Charlie. 'It's because he wouldn't have the patience to sit there long enough.'

'I 'eard that,' said Vernon, increasing the speed as they left the moored boats behind.
They passed through two bridge holes then entered a stretch with tall reed beds on either side.
Linda told Charlie that they were home to a wealth of bird and water life, like toads and dragonflies.
Vernon added that sedge warblers nest in the reeds.
Linda looked at him, surprised that he knew that.
Charlie kept the tiller bar straight as the boat slid through the narrow-overgrown channel.

'This is where we don't want to meet a wide beam coming towards us,' said Vernon.
Gradually the reeds lessoned and the canal widened once more. A small wharf on the port side had been converted into a private home, complete with their own narrowboat moored alongside.

The final bridge hole before the pub moorings carried a lane to a local village, a group of cyclists dressed in orange and black tops had stopped to watch the boat pass underneath. Charlie tooted the horn, they waved.

'Right, I'd better take the tiller,' said Vernon, 'in case we have to fit into a tight spot.'
As luck would have it a boat, longer than theirs, was leaving the mooring just as they exited the bridge. 'That'll do us,' chuckled Vernon, pointing the bow towards the bank. He reduced speed and

glided the boat alongside. Linda jumped off with the bow line, and Charlie with the stern. Once the boat was securely moored, they locked it up and walked the short distance along the lane to the pub.

Vernon and Linda were regular visitors and knew the staff and other customers well. Charlie sat on one of the tall stools next to the bar.

'So how are you young Charlie? asked the landlord,

'I've just steered all the way from the marina,' said Charlie.

'Wow, that's something,' he replied, handing him a large glass of fresh orange juice.

Vernon took a long drink from his pint of beer. 'Ah that's good,' he said smacking his lips together. He placed his hand on Charlie's head. 'I have to say he did really well. I was surprised.'

'Told you,' said Charlie. 'William taught me how to steer.'

The landlord asked who William was. Charlie was just about to explain when Linda interrupted.

'I think we'll just have the menus please.'

CHAPTER SIXTEEN

The Three-Legged Mare

The engine of the trip boat was not as bad as Wilf had expected so he agreed to schedule it in the following week. Although it wasn't yet summer a few people were sitting at the small round tables in the front garden of the Toll House. Wilf waved goodbye to Maggie as she came out of the house carrying a large, brown, china tea pot. No sooner had your cup emptied than she was there with a refill. Ken, not being needed had returned to his gardening. The two golden retrievers barked at Wilf from behind the gate.

As he walked back down the flight his thoughts returned once again to the white van man. He could just confront him and ask what he was doing parked there, but it wasn't his land, so he had no authority to do that. Did he work? If so, doing what and where? Maybe it was just a homeless guy living in his van. Even so it still seemed too coincidental that he was parked there when the three robberies had taken place. On reaching the bottom lock before the marina he sat on the balance beam and took out a cigarette. The grey mackerel clouds had parted, and a splash of thin sunshine washed across his face. He went back through the gate and into the small field where the grazing sheep had now moved to the crest. As he climbed over the stile, a car was driving into the hire boat car park.

Wilf could access the marina that way, so he followed them through and closed the gate after them.

A tall middle-aged man stepped from the driver's door of the new Audi Avant car. 'Thanks for doing the gate.'

'No problem', said Wilf. 'You going out on one of the hire boats?' The man replied that they were taking a week's early spring break. He laughed. 'We needed to get away from London.' Wilf nodded. 'I can understand that.'

His wife and two children had got out of the car. 'We lost our dog a few weeks ago,' said the woman. The man interrupted. 'Another reason to get away, change of scenery.'

'How long had you had him?' asked Wilf.

The man smiled and pointed to the two children. 'Longer than those two.' Wilf guessed they were early teens.

'I'd better get on,' said Wilf. 'Have a good trip.' As they started to unload the car the man called out. 'I take it the car is safe in here?' Wilf nodded. 'No prob mate.'

The food was always good at the Three-Legged Mare and today was no exception. Vernon didn't do puddings, Linda and Charlie did, finishing their meal off with homemade apple pie and custard. Vernon settled for another couple of pints before they left. Walking back to the boat Charlie felt he was going to explode. 'I won't need any more to eat for a week,' he said to Linda.

She smiled. 'Yeah right.'

A small lane ran alongside the pub towards the towpath. On one side were old cottages. On the other was a sizeable camp site and caravan park that seemed to be busy all year round, which was good news for the brewery who owned the Three-Legged Mare. When they reached the boat, another vessel had moored astern of them. Charlie thought the man sitting on the cruiser stern looked weird. He had long hair that almost reached his waist, and a white beard. It reminded Charlie of a wizard. He wore a black top hat with a long blue coat. His trousers seemed to be made of lots of different squares of coloured cloth and his shoes were bright green. Vernon and Linda knew him.

'Allo Mickey,' said Vernon. 'Long time no see.'

Linda whispered to Charlie. 'That's Magic Mickey, he's a magician, of sorts.'

'Who's this then?' Mickey asked.

'This is our grandson, Charlie,' replied Linda.

'Nice to meet you Charlie,' said Mickey. 'Do you like magic?'

Charlie shrugged. 'Don't know really.'

Micky took a pack of cards from his pocket and shuffled them.

'Take a card,' he said. 'Don't show it to me.'

Charlie pulled one out, looked at it and held it in his hand.

'Now put it back in the pack,' said Mickey, looking away. He shuffled the pack again then pulled a black and white wand from an inside pocket. He tapped the stack of cards three times. Charlie watched him closely. Suddenly he threw all the cards into the air, except one which he kept between his fingers. He turned it over and showed it to Charlie. 'Your card I believe young man.' Charlies eyes widened with disbelief. 'How did you do that?' he asked.

Mickey laughed. 'Tricks of the trade young man, tricks of the trade.'

Vernon and Linda had seen them all before, but still didn't know how he did it.

'How's things in the marina?' asked Mickey. 'I heard you had some pilfering.'

Linda was just about to ask how he knew, when, anticipating her question, he laughed loudly.

'Jungle drums,' he said. 'You can't keep anything secret on the cut.'

She knew that but would have preferred it to have been kept quiet.

'We've got to be away,' said Vernon. 'We'll see you at the weekend.'

'Look forward to it,' called Mickey, as they went aboard their boat.

To turn around at the winding hole they would need to go through the swing bridge.

'All yours Charlie,' said Vernon.

It was only a short distance along the canal to the swing bridge. In a field which ascended towards a packed tree line, inquisitive Huacaya

Alpaca idly roamed alongside the waterside hedgerow. Charlie had never seen these creatures before and asked Linda what they were. They had to go slow as several narrowboats were moored against the grassy bank on the opposite side. The water being shallow the boaters had to use the brow to step ashore. Vernon complained that they should build more hard standing moorings, particularly as it was such a popular place for boats to stop.

Vernon controlled the throttle as Charlie glided the boat next to the hard standing jetty adjacent to the swing bridge. Linda jumped off and tied the midline to a mooring ring. Vernon handed her the windlass. She would need this to undo the locknut and chain that secured the bridge to the opposite bank. After unscrewing it she pushed on the long steel arm and slowly the bridge started to open. Vernon released the midline, pushed off and jumped on.

'So did William show you how to turn the boat around Charlie?' asked Vernon.
Charlie shook his head. 'No, we never had to do that.'

As they passed through the open bridge into the winding hole Vernon gave a little tweak to the throttle. 'Right tiller hard over Charlie,' he said, 'and keep an eye on the bow as it comes round.' When the bow had stopped swinging, he quickly put the engine into reverse and told Charlie to push the tiller bar the other way, after one more forward manoeuvre they were ready to go back through the bridge.

'Good stuff Charlie!' said Vernon, patting him on the shoulder. They moored alongside the hardstanding whilst Linda closed the bridge behind them. On the journey back Vernon told Charlie that he now believed William had taught him boat handling. Charlie smiled as he remembered his time on Speculator with William, Ma Hams, and Thunder, and wondered if he would ever see them again.

It was early evening when they arrived back. Before reaching the marina, Charlie had succumbed to tiredness and crashed out on the sofa down below. Once again moored alongside the ranch building, Linda and Vernon joined him in the cabin. After a much-needed mug of tea, they too were soon asleep in the chairs.

Bert was fiddling with the coffee machine in the ranch building.

'It's not working,' Alex called from the office. 'You'll have to drink instant.'
Bert pulled a face and muttered something under his breath. 'There's only instant,' he shouted across to Jeb and Bruce. Jeb was reading a newspaper that somebody else had left, he refused to buy one. Bruce was checking social media on his smart phone. They both gave a thumbs up to indicate that it was ok. It wasn't alright with Bert though, he detested instant coffee and objected having to pay for it.
Bert returned with three cups of coffee, put them on the table and sat down in a huff.

'What's up with you?' asked Jeb.

'That's the second time that bloody machine's broken down,' he grumbled. 'They should get a new one.'

Bruce looked up from his phone. 'You've got plenty of money, you could donate one.'

Bert spluttered into his coffee. 'Me,' he shouted. 'Why should I pay for one?'

'Well, you're one of the biggest users,' replied Bruce.

'What about you?' retorted Bert. 'You're always in 'ere.'

Bruce shrugged. 'Yeah, but I don't complain when it goes wrong.'

Bert was just about to continue arguing, when Jeb interrupted him. 'Will you two shut up about the damn coffee. Look at this,' he said, showing them the headlines in the newspaper.

'This Corona Virus thing is getting really serious, it's not just in China, they reckon it's spreading across other countries.'

'Well it won't come here will it?' said Bert. 'We're on an island.'

Jeb and Bruce looked at each other in disbelief.

'It is here,' said Jeb. 'Apparently people are already showing symptoms.'

'Bloody Chinese,' said Bert, rolling a cigarette. 'I wouldn't trust 'em any further than I could throw 'em. Look what they're doing in Hong Kong. Just like that Putin fella, and those Olioiks buying up Britain with their mafia money.'

166

'He's Russian, 'said Bruce, 'and it's Oligarchs.'

Jeb interrupted. 'It's Greek; means 'Rule by the few.'

Bert snorted. 'Well that proves my point and I know 'es bloody Russian. They're all in on it.'

'In on what?' asked Jeb laughing.

'World domination,' said Bert. 'That's what these buggers are after.'

Bruce shook his head. 'Not another one of your conspiracy theories.'

'You wait and see,' said Bert, standing up. 'I'll be proved right.'

Vernon heard the tail end of the conversation as he and Charlie came into the ranch building from the veranda. 'Proved right about what?' asked Vernon.

Jeb shook his head. 'Don't ask, he's away with the fairies.'

'I'm going home today,' said Charlie. 'My mum's picking me up this afternoon.'

Bruce asked if he had enjoyed himself.

He nodded. 'It's been great. And I got to steer the boat to the pub and back.'

'He did good,' added Vernon. 'William taught him well.'

Jeb said, 'We heard all about your dream, must be great to be able to go back in time like that.'

Charlie replied. 'It wasn't a dream, it was real.'

Jeb smiled, envious of childhood imagination. 'I'm sure it was Charlie, you hold on to that memory, it's very special.'

Bert finished his cigarette and stubbed it out on the gravelled surface, then went back inside.

'Charlie's off,' said Bruce.

Bert laughed. 'I wondered what that smell was.' His attempt at humour was lost on Charlie.

'See you again,' said Bert, holding his hand out for Charlie to shake.

He was just about to sit down again when Mur appeared at the door clutching a supermarket bag for life. 'You ready?' she said.

He raised his eyebrows. 'Bloody shopping. Pain in the arse.'

'Listen to him,' said Mur. 'All he has to do is push the trolley, and he complains about that.'

Bert snorted and reluctantly followed her to the car park.

Jeb chuckled. 'I don't know how she puts up with him.'

Bruce said. 'They probably wouldn't be happy if they weren't arguing all the time.'

Alex called to Charlie from the office.

Vernon made a tea and sat down with Bruce and Jeb.

'I spoke to Wilf last night,' said Vernon. 'He was saying that Ken's getting concerned he might be made redundant and they sell off the Toll House.'

Jeb shook his head. 'Nothing would ever surprise me. People don't seem to be interested in boaters even though we're the one's paying a licence fee.'

'So, what would they do then?' asked Bruce.

'No, idea,' replied Vernon. 'They'd have to rent somewhere.'

'Bloody disgrace,' said Jeb, 'after all the years he and his family have lived there.'

Charlie arrived back with a bar of chocolate that Alex had given him. Tazz, Alex's spaniel, sat drooling in expectation of a piece. 'You can't have chocolate, silly dog,' said Charlie.

CHAPTER SEVENTEEN

From Little Acorns

Tyler was feeling incredibly pleased with himself as he slipped his full wallet into his back pocket.

'See you soon,' his mate had said as the young man stepped out into the dark from the crowded Green Man pub. He could always rely on Budgie to shift his gear. Being the same age, they had known each other since school where they had honed their 'craft'. Both regarded their currant lifestyle as a preferable alternative to earning an honest living. He was a chancer, a ducker and diver who never planned anything, instead relying on those 'quick nicks' as he called them, which presented themselves everywhere.

He had parked his white van in a car park behind some shops, a short walk from the crowded pub. Zipping up his jacket he wandered slowly back along the narrow street, occasionally stopping to look in the shop windows. Puffing on his vape he blew a cloud of strawberry and cream flavoured smoke into the night air. He had been away from this area now for four days, enough time to have visited his other lucrative haunts in various parts of the county. Smiling, he thought of how easy people made it for him to rob them, and as for the police, theft was way down on their agenda. Besides most people were insured, so what the hell.

There was a car parked next to the van. He looked inside, force of habit. An expensive looking bag was sitting in the passenger side footwell. He was tempted, it would be an easy nick, but it was too risky in a public place. He hadn't evaded being caught for so long by being careless. Opening the driver's door of the van he slid behind the steering wheel, put on the seat belt and turned the ignition key. The cold engine spluttered and shook before eventually starting.

He had asked Budgie to find someone to service it. He chuckled. It would probably be the same bloke who had given him a bent MOT last year. Not that he was complaining.

Turning out onto the road that he had just walked down he checked the time on the dashboard clock. It was just gone ten. 'Perfect,' he thought, nobody would see him arrive and park.

He passed through the historic market square, now empty of cars, then crossed over the canal where the top lock sits beneath the road bridge. Soon he was at the foot of the long hill, where the dual carriageway narrowed into two-way traffic.

The entrance to the marina was only a short distance away. He knew it well having been here many times before. The part asphalt track snaked its way between caliginous fields and farm buildings, before turning sharply onto a downward slope that ran past the bubble. Two small rabbits sat at the edge watching his approach, then turned and ran in different directions towards the hedgerow. In the distance he could see the illuminated windows of moored craft and beyond the streetlamps of the main road. His headlights picked up the closed high security gates of the marina. Before reaching them, he pulled off onto a patch of rough ground that ran alongside. The loose stones and gravel crunched under the wheels of the van as he turned towards the tall hedge and stopped.

Alan had been out since morning. He eased back the accelerator of the 1980 green classic MG B Cabriolet as he approached the sharp double bend opposite the Black Horse pub. Recently purchased, this was his latest expensive toy, along with the 'beast', his 1000cc motorcycle. On the way back to the marina he had called at the Toll House to see Ken. As a fellow motorcyclist he had an interest in Ken's classic bike collection, often helping him with the ongoing renovation.

He changed to a lower gear as he followed a slow-moving tractor towing a trailer full of hay, then when the opportunity arose, he pressed down on the accelerator pedal and quickly overtook it. The gates to the marina were opened, but before passing through he noticed that the white van was again parked alongside. The MG was kept in the small carpark just inside the marina entrance, which gave Alan plenty of room to 'groom' and tinker with it. He pulled up next to Jimmy's Land Rover and switched off the engine. As he stepped out, a voice from behind startled him.

'Afternoon, Lewis Hamilton.' Turning round, a large black wolf's head butted into his groin. Alan stroked Zeke and laughed. 'He nearly did some damage there.'

'Good drive?' asked Allison, pulling Zeke back besides her.

Alan nodded. 'Went for a spin across the plain, certainly blew the cobwebs away.'

'I heard things aren't too good between Luke and Ryan.'

Alan shook his head. 'I think they're getting better, no thanks to that bloody Rita stirring the pot.'

'It's not the first time she's caused trouble,' said Allison.

'Why people can't just mind their own business is beyond me,' he replied.

Allison shrugged, before walking off with Zeke. 'What goes round comes round,' she called.

Leaving the car, he walked back to his boat for a cloth to wipe it down with. Jock was sitting at the wooden table on the strip of grass between the pontoons and the hedge.

'There's a can of beer with your name on here,' he said.

'Sounds good,' Alan replied, joining him. Judging by the number of empty cans on the floor Jock had been there for some time.

'You alright mate?' he asked, sensing a pensive mood.

Jock nodded. 'I've just been watching the news. This bloody Corona Virus is getting dodgy, they're now saying people are panic buying in the supermarkets.'

Alan took a swig of the cold beer. 'We better get a stock in then,' he said, holding up the can, 'before they sell out.'

Jock chuckled. 'It's not beer they're hoarding mate, it's toilet rolls.'

'Why, does it give you the runs?' asked Alan. Jock shrugged. 'No idea mate,' he laughed. 'I've got plenty of newspaper though, if it does.'

At the canal edge
Daffodils sway upon the breeze
The yellow trumpets of early spring
Wild and bold against winter's waning stare

The grass had started to grow, small clumps of bright and cheerful daisies are scattered upon the ground like thrown confetti. A wash of wild Narcissus yellow covers un-trod verges and otherwise neglected corners of the marina. Vernon didn't appreciate nature's gentle awakening as it meant he would have to regularly mow the grass on his antiquated machine. Vernon didn't do regularity, preferring a more ad hoc approach to his working day, often much to Linda's frustration.

The following morning Alan whistled as he and Peter walked from their boats to the ranch for a coffee. The drive in his MG Cabriolet the previous day had lifted his mood, which at times could be quite dark and troubled. Lennie was coming from the opposite direction.

'You look all in mate,' said Peter.
Lennie nodded. 'I am. It was a push getting that boat finished yesterday, and I've got another one coming in today.'

'I see our friend in the van is back,' said Alan.

'Yeah, we'll need to watch him,' he replied, before walking off to start work.

'He still thinks it's him then?' asked Peter. Alan shook his head. 'So does Wilf, though I'm not so sure. Have you heard any more about your missing wallet?'

'Not a dicky bird,' he replied, 'and I don't think Lewis and Jodie have either.'

'It would have been different in my day,' said Alan. 'We were thief takers, not bloody social workers.'

When they reached the ranch building Vernon was hovering anxiously by the door.

'You waiting for something?' asked Alan.

'Heavy plant,' he replied abruptly.

Peter laughed. 'What's that then, a giant cactus?' There was no reply.

Inside, Jeb, Sid and Hazel were pawing over a map of the waterways. She and Sid had decided to leave the marina earlier than planned and accompany Jeb on the journey north, which would make life easier for him being single handed.

'When are you off?' Alan asked Jeb.

'Next Wednesday, all being well,' he replied.

Alan laughed. 'Early mornings and late nights then, it's a long haul.' He knew this route well as he and Vernon had recently brought a narrowboat back to the marina from the midlands.

Hazel chuckled. 'Not likely. I don't do early mornings, and it's me who will end up doing the locks.'

Sid nodded, 'She will. Tell 'em about the time you got your bosom caught in the paddle gear.'

Again, there was a loud guffaw before she recounted the story. 'I was showing some people, who were clearly new to boating, how to wind up the lock paddles. Then my blouse got caught in the ratchet and I couldn't get it out.'

Sid added, 'She was yacking and not paying attention.'

'What did you do then?' asked Peter.
She shrugged. 'There was no choice. I had to undress, revealing all.'

'Christ,' laughed Alan, 'that was an eyeful for the onlookers.'
Hazel chuckled. 'It was bloody embarrassing, particularly with fulsome boobies like mine.'
Sid said dryly, 'She's lucky it wasn't her tongue.'

That vision had left Jeb in need of a smoke. He went outside where Vernon was watching the long vehicle as it crept cautiously into the marina, its rear wheels occasionally running over the white painted stones that lined the edge. It came to a halt outside the ranch building, blocking the access road. The driver, a short stout man with a florid complexion, wearing soiled green overalls, jumped down from the cab. Vernon went to meet him. On the back of the trailer was a dumper truck, a roller and a small digger all hired from a local plant hire firm. A few days earlier a large pile of crushed

176

aggregate had been deposited alongside the grass in the Ranch Sector. This was to be 'Operation Hole Fill' prompted by the recent mysterious disappearance of several small people, into large potholes. Vernon showed the driver where to off-load them and returned to the building, clutching paperwork to be signed.

'That's going to keep you busy,' said Alan. Vernon sniffed. He clearly was not enthused by the forthcoming task.

Rita had been lurking in the corner of the room eager to pick up on any morsel of casual conversation that she could translate into juicy gossip. At first, she attempted to engage with Alan, who showed little interest in exchanging small talk with her, especially after the Ryan and Luke affair. Eventually, sensing the cool mood towards her, she finished drinking her tea and departed.

Being more left of centre than Alan when it came to compassion, Peter did have a scintilla of sympathy for the woman. He appreciated what it was like to be one of the 7.7 million living alone, many not out of choice. Not that either of them was a troglodyte, but there were only so many times you could escape daytime television or self-reflection in search of social interaction with others. Although, unlike her, he did subscribe to the view that if you must beat yourself up, then do not do it to other people.

Hazel, who had wandered into the office to speak with Linda about their departure, returned to the table with a coffee and a giant Eccles cake.

Alan chuckled. 'That company will go broke when you leave here.'

She emitted a loud rebounding guffaw. 'I'll soon find another supplier up there.'

Tyler had been on a reconnaissance. He had already earmarked several possibilities for a 'quick nick'; boats moored against the towpath, parked cars, a mobile home and even an empty cottage in a nearby village. Arriving back, he opened the back doors of the white van, took out a can of cola, and downed it in one, this was followed by a meat pasty, and although being suspicious of the 'use by' date he ate it anyway. His sleeping bag was laid out on top of a thick length of foam. He crawled inside and lay down. Now all he had to do was decide which job to do and when.

Earlier in the morning his sleep had been disturbed when a long low loader carrying a new wide beam boat had reversed and parked next to him on the spare ground. He had waited for someone to bang on the van and ask why he was there, but no one did.

Soon afterwards another heavy vehicle arrived with a huge yellow crane on it. He ate some bread and ham, drank a pint of milk and walked down to watch the operation of lifting the heavy boat off the trailer and into the canal. At one point it swung free like an alien UFO preparing to land.

'No room for error there,' he thought, equating it to his own activities.

Several people had gathered to watch the launch, and still no one asked who he was, which struck him as odd as he assumed most people would have known each other.

Alongside the van was a row of tangled trees that bounded the marina. The branches, whilst in bud, were yet to yield their fulsome summer coat. Tyler, keen to monitor the movements of people in and around the marina, had observed through the semi naked limbs as Alan had carefully wiped down the gleaming classic car. A plan started to formulate in his mind. That was an expensive piece of kit and could be sold on quickly for a good price. He puffed on his vape as Alan finished sprucing up the MG before finally securing the cover over the interior. Tyler watched which boat he went back to. He chuckled to himself, 'Easy peasy,' but he would need an accomplice, and who better at nicking cars than Budgie. He took out his phone and called him.

CHAPTER EIGHTEEN

Retribution

Before Vernon and Alex could be let loose on the expensive and potentially dangerous hired plant machinery, they would be required to complete a two-day on-site training course. Although a health and safety stipulation, imposed by the marina owners Vernon, being an ex HGV driver of some years, was not happy at this 'being taught to suck eggs' imposition. Alex on the other hand, being ex-military and used to bullshit, as ever took it all in his stride.

It was obvious from the arrival of the instructor, a punctilious character bearing a very thick training manual, that his relationship with Vernon would be a fraught one. He was a methodical man who was determined that every 'i' should be dotted twice, and every 't' crossed thrice. This enforced and time-consuming rigor irritated Vernon even more, regarding him as pompous.

After an initial briefing where Vernon struggled to stay awake, they left the ranch building wearing yellow safety hats and high viz jackets. Frequent shouts of, 'There goes Bob the Builder,' from fellow boaters were ignored. Following another 'on site' safety talk and a close inspection of the three bright yellow vehicles, they were eventually allowed to climb up and sit in one. Vernon's phone rang, which resulted in a disapproving look from the instructor, he did not answer it.

The remainder of the day was spent practicing loading and re-loading, dumping, and re-dumping, endlessly changing different size buckets on the digger and driving the roller back and forth over the same piece of ground. All of this was under the critical eye of the captain who was quick to point out the slightest error of judgement and admonish accordingly. Even a sudden prolonged heavy downpour did nothing to deflect him from his exhaustive training schedule.

'All the boxes have to be ticked,' he would insist, tapping his pen on the top of the clipboard.

At the end of the first day Vernon was ready to carry out an act of violence on the man, using expletives in the ranch building that would have shocked any seasoned naval matelot. Fortunately, he had left for his hotel before this pent-up eruption took place, and Linda was the only one who heard it.

The second day would be a repeat of the first, though with higher expectations. The morning briefing included a recap of the previous day's learning experiences and a Health and Safety question and answer. Alex shared Vernon's disdain for this 'nanny society' approach to risk but he stayed quiet. Vernon on the other hand did little to disguise his antipathy.

By the afternoon the obsessive box ticker, who was nearing the bottom of his long list, was complementing both men on their newly acquired handling, digging, dumping, and rolling skills. Even Vernon, albeit begrudgingly, had to admit that he had learnt something and improved. An appraisal of their individual performances followed in the ranch where he extolled the virtues of a good teacher and willing student relationship.

The following week both men, minus their Bob the Builder yellow hats and clutching their recent accreditation certificates, embarked on 'Operation Hole Fill' around the marina. It took a long time, but eventually the tall pile of crushed aggregate had been reduced to a wide patch of pink coloured dust on the ground, and the track was once more navigably acceptable. Both men rightly congratulated themselves on a job well done, though Vernon was still adamant that he could have done it without such laborious instruction.

Unfortunately, in a few months, history would repeat itself, and despite Vernon and Alex's herculean effort, it would be like the biblical parable of the man who built his house on the sand. One big wave, or in this case heavy prolonged rain would see the crushed aggregate washed away, and once more the vertically challenged would be in danger of disappearing into a big hole, never to be seen again.

When Tyler met Budgie in the Green Man public house, they had already agreed a plan of action. On the far side of town was a small industrial estate where Budgie had a lockup. It was to here that they would bring the stolen MG car.

Budgie had already spoken to several of his local contacts and anticipated a quick sale. They left the pub at closing time and wandered to a neighbouring street where Budgie's favourite take away Kebab shop was. There was no hurry.

The bright lights of the shop contrasted with the darkened street. It was busy, but that was nothing unusual after the pubs turned out. Budgie knew several of the people queuing, most of them local villains, or small-time drug dealers. They ordered two Doner kebabs with chilli sauce, then walked back to Tyler's white van parked in the market square. The town clock struck midnight. Two drunken men staggered into the square, one stopped and urinated close to the war memorial.

'Bloody pond life,' said Budgie. 'No respect.' Tyler smiled at the irony.

'Did you get the gate code?' asked Budgie. He nodded. 'Course, I just waited until someone came along, then told 'em I was making a delivery, and they gave it to me.'
Budgie laughed. 'Too trusting, some people.'

Tyler passed a can of cola to Budgie. 'We'll give it half an hour and then get going.'
A slow-moving police car passed by the square. Budgie watched as it disappeared down the high street, then wound the window down and lit a cigarette.

'So, 'ow much we gonna make on the wheels?' Tyler asked.
Budgie thought for a moment. 'Anything up to 20k, I reckon.'

'Not bad for a night's work,' he smiled, checking the time on his phone.

Budgie nodded. 'Keep the wolves from the door.'

Tyler turned the ignition key. 'It's time,' he said.

Lennie couldn't sleep. He sat up in bed and turned on the small reading light above his head.

His mind flitted between thoughts like a butterfly in a breeze. Toby, his small terrier who was asleep next to him emitted a low growl of protest at being disturbed. Lennie threw back the duvet and stepped from the bed. He turned on the television, not that he anticipated finding anything worth watching at one o'clock in the morning. Switching on the kettle he looked out across a darkened marina. A lone light shone from the window of a boat on the far side. He smiled. 'Another person who couldn't sleep.'

Whilst sipping from his mug of tea he flicked lazily through the television channels and their mind numbing offerings. Eventually he got bored and switched it off. He pulled on a pair of shorts and a coat then poked Toby.

'Come on you lazy hound, let's go for a walk.' The little dog yawned and reluctantly jumped off the bed. Outside, the pontoon was damp from an earlier shower. He attached Toby's lead to his collar then went past the ranch building to the grassy bank opposite. The low cloud and quarter moon had cast an inky black veil across the marina.

He stopped, took out his vape and immersed himself in this nocturnal world.

Tyler extinguished the headlights as he coasted the white van down the slope in front of the marina entrance. Both he and Budgie turned off their phones before leaving the vehicle. The job would not require tools, just a quick hot wire and they would be away, and considerably richer.
Tyler smiled. They had certainly picked the right night, 'black as Newgate's locker,' as his old man used to say. Not that it had done him much good, he was doing three years in prison for nicking lead off a church roof. There was a wooden post with a keypad at the side of the high security gates. He entered the four-digit code and the gates slowly opened. It was not difficult to find the MG classic amongst the other parked cars; it was the only one with an open top.

Budgie switched on his narrow beam LED torch. Tyler undid the cover and rolled it back. An owl hooted to the night. Tyler spooked by the sudden noise strained his eyes through the gloom to make sure they were alone. Budgie swore.

'What's up man?' asked Tyler.

'It's got a bloody steering lock on,' he whispered.
Tyler punched the side of the car. 'Shit, can you get it off?'

Budgie nodded. 'Yeah, it's a good one though, attached to the pedals. I'll need my bag from the van'. The reply from Tyler was impatient and abrupt. 'Go then bruv, just be quick.' He leant against the car as Budgie disappeared into the night.

The long-grassed bank tapered out near the car park. Lennie and Toby had followed the tree line, occasionally stopping to allow the little dog to root in the undergrowth. It was as he was about to turn around that Lennie heard the gates open. He stood quietly on the damp grass until they had closed. 'That's odd,' he whispered to Toby, 'there's nobody there.' Toby did not answer.

He was just deciding whether to explore further when the gates re-opened. Picking up the dog in case he barked he took a step back into the shadow of the tree line. As the gates again closed, he could just make out a figure walking towards the car park. He was carrying something, but Lennie wasn't sure what. In normal circumstances, whilst unusual, it would not have prompted suspicion, but with the recent spate of thefts and the nearby presence of the white van Lennie smelt a large rat.

Having demolished two bottles of his favourite red wine Alan and Wilf had fallen asleep on the sofa whilst watching a box set. At first Alan thought he was dreaming, then waking with a start he grabbed at the smart phone that was emitting a shrill intrusive noise into his befuddled brain.

'Alan, it's Lennie,' he said softly. 'I think our man is in the car park.'
Alan could hardly hear him. 'What? What man? Where are you?' he asked sleepily.

Lennie raised his voice as loud as he dared. 'For Christ sake wake up mate. Meet me in the car park and stay out of sight.'

He shook Wilf who was snoring loudly, then staggered to the sink and splashed cold water on his face. Wilf opened his eyes and yawned. 'What up mate?' he asked blurrily. Alan urgently relayed the call from Lennie.

Walking unsteadily along the pontoon the cold night air slammed into them both. Suddenly the implication hit Alan, what if it was his car they were after. They quickened their step making sure not to be seen. Reaching the end of the pontoon, Alan stopped and texted Lennie. 'Where are U?' The reply came back. 'B hind sheds, UR car. Meet @ gate.'

Between the car park and the next pontoon was another wide grass strip. Alan crept silently along the far edge with the moored boats behind him. As he neared the access road into the marina, he heard the soft purring of the MG's engine. 'Christ they've got it started,' he thought. A wave of anger washed through him.

Budgie sat with both hands on the wooden steering wheel. 'Nice motor.'
Tyler was panicking. It had taken longer than expected to get it started. 'Let's get out of 'ere,' he said. 'I'll open the gates, see you at the lockup.' He ran across the car park to where the wooden post stood. His outstretched hand never reached the green exit button on the post. The heavy blow from somewhere in the dark knocked him sideways into

a bush. With blood streaming from his nose he felt himself being dragged around the corner onto the moist grass with Toby snapping at his ankles. Then someone was kneeling on his chest with their hand across his mouth. He struggled to get free but to no avail.

Budgie released the handbrake and put the car into gear. He smiled as he thought of this nice little earner. The gates were still closed. 'Tyler,' he called softly. 'Where are yer?' Before any answer was forthcoming the driver's door was suddenly pulled open and Budgie, who had omitted to wear the seat belt, was hauled violently from the car. He felt an excruciating pain down below as Alan's knee thundered into his groin, bent double, a punch to the side of his head sent him sprawling onto the ground.

'I'm round 'ere,' Lennie called.
Alan hauled Budgie to his feet and marched him to where Lennie was standing over the whimpering and bleeding Tyler.

Wilf took a torch from his pocket. 'So, what two scroats have we got here then?' he said, shining the beam across their frightened faces. The 'gentle' interrogation during the next hour revealed their involvement not only in the recent boat thefts, but further afield. Wilf demanded all the money they had on them. Any reluctance was soon dispelled after he threatened to phone the police. Budgie reluctantly pulled from his pocket a wedge of notes secured with an elastic band. Tyler was equally forthcoming, his wallet containing over one hundred pounds.

It took little persuasion, with a threat of the consequences, for the men to agree never to return to this area. They considered themselves fortunate not be in handcuffs, although Lennie, who himself had had brushes with the 'old bill' in the past had no interest in turning them in. The three men escorted the dejected youngsters out of the marina to where their white van was parked.

'You wanna get that nose seen to, looks like it's broken,' chuckled Lennie, as Tyler lowered himself painfully into the driver's seat. They watched as the van disappeared up the track.

'I don't think we'll be seeing them again,' said Alan.

Wilf nodded. 'Not if they've got any sense, bloody chancers.'

CHAPTER NINETEEN

Strange Times

After dispatching the white van and its unhappy occupants Alan moved the car back to its parking space. He checked the interior for damage using Wilf's torch. Apart from the steering lock there was none. He replaced the cover. 'I think we deserve a nightcap after that,' he said laughing.

Neither man felt the need to inform anyone in the marina about the incident, particularly Linda and Vernon. Lennie was concerned that it would prompt more questions than they had the answers to. After all, there was no damage to the car, and they had recovered over three hundred pounds, no doubt acquired by the pair through ill-gotten gains.

Alan had rightly pointed out, that there was no direct evidence linking either man to any of the boat thefts, so there was little point in having them arrested for attempting to steal a car, and they would only get a slap on the wrist. Wilf, fortifying himself with a large glass of Alan's Jameson's whisky, laughed when suggesting that their use of 'reasonable force' when extracting confessions might also be questioned.

Dawn had broken by the time Lennie and Wilf left Alan's boat. As Lennie went back across the marina to his boat, a milky blue, orange streaked sky was pushing aside the night's gloom. Swimming alongside the pontoon Ronnie, the ever-thuggish swan, hissed menacingly at Toby as he and Lennie walked along it. A muffled bark came from inside Alex's boat as they passed. On the main road outside, Lennie could hear the steady build-up of early morning traffic as it sped by on its way into town. At the darkened ranch building the slack halyards chatted loudly as they slapped against the metal flag poles. He took out his vape, for one last puff before going inside the boat. A low mist hugged the still water. Two gulls swooped noisily overhead, and a donkey brayed loudly in a distant field. He did not bother going back to bed, instead falling asleep in the chair with Toby on his lap.

Peter and Jodie never did expect to hear any more about the money taken from their boats. She had given up collecting coins in a jar and he was always careful in future to lock the doors when leaving his boat, although it still galled him to do so. It was therefore with some surprise that weeks later they had each received a mystery envelope containing the exact amount that had gone missing. A brief handwritten note inside said, 'From a well-wisher.' Despite trying, they never did discover who that person was.

The elderly couple who had been broken into on the towpath near the marina were moored on the Thames at Windsor. They had just returned from a visit to the castle when they received a phone call asking for their postal address, though Alan did have to tell Linda a little white lie to get their number. After learning of the incident their well-meaning children did again try to persuade them to sell the boat and move back to the house in Derby. The friendship they had received at Crockenhill Marina though, had hardened their resolve to stay afloat and be part of this boating community for as long as they could.

Little did those who gathered for the marina spring Air Ambulance fund raising event realise that this would be the last time they or countless others, would gather for a social event for many weeks or months. Outside the ranch building different coloured gazebos had been erected on the gravelled surface, tables and chairs laid out and the barbeque prepared for the evening. Coloured bunting flew above and huge speakers for the band were set up in each corner. After several weeks of chilled winds and rain, sunshine was spreading itself extravagantly across the marina, promising a nice day and lifting everybody's mood.

This event was also to be a farewell to Jeb who was leaving shortly to travel to a new marina near Milton Keynes. He would be missed especially by Bruce and Bert, who secretly believed and hoped that he would get so far and turn back, something he had done before. Alan, Peter, Archie and the other band members had been practising every Thursday afternoon in the ranch building putting together an impressive repertoire of songs, no mean feat considering the relatively short time they had been playing together, and other liquid distractions.

A bouncy castle had been booked for visiting children. Unfortunately, it failed to arrive. At a previous event it had blown into an adjoining field sustaining serious damage when landing amongst a herd of bemused cows. Bert had made some inappropriate remark about the kids still being in it, which resulted in Mur throwing a book at him.

One shaded table groaned under the weight of two barrels of real ale purchased from a local microbrewery. Linda had some scepticism regarding Vernon's self-appointed role as head barman, reinforcing the concept to him that he was there to sell it, not consume it. To be sure she had asked Bruce to work alongside him. Vernon had looked quite hurt at the accusation of such impropriety.

Magic Mickey had cycled the short distance from his mooring by the Three-Legged Mare. He arrived on a yellow bike towing a small metal trailer wearing a red fez with an army camouflage jacket. His multi coloured trousers and green shoes were the same as when Vernon, Charlie and Linda had last seen him. Linda found him a table under a small gazebo, and he laid out his props for his magic show in the afternoon. Earlier in the week he had asked Jock to help him perform some tricks on the day. He was reluctant at first but after a few pints agreed.

As a proud Scot Jock was, as usual, wearing his kilt. If asked, he would point out that it was the tartan of Clan Macdonald who had fought alongside Bonnie Prince Charlie against the British at the battle of Culloden in 1746. However even a descendant of these fearsome highland warriors was wary of what the unpredictable Magic Mickey might ask him to do.

In the ranch building three tables were stacked with squishy and tempting homemade cakes and biscuits donated by moorers. Mur and Julia had combined their talents to produce a variety of savoury flans and pies. Eva and Jodie had organised the raffle and had spent weeks twisting people's arms in and around the town for prizes.

The sign pinned to the front of the table said, 'Madame Zara. Fortune Telling and Tarot Card Readings.' Although a serious medium and spiritual healer, Glenda adopted this stage name for such fun events as this. A purple cloth adorned with moons and stars covered the surface of the table. A round upturned glass bowl stood in the middle covered by a white cloth and on a chair stood a portable CD player, emitting eerie underwater whale sounds. Glenda or 'Madame Zara' wore a long-coloured headscarf and a flowing flowery skirt, a gold ring hung from each ear.

Jimmy and Lewis were to oversee the tug of war which was to be held on the wide grass bank, alongside the access road. There was some concern as to whether it would take place at all, as a suitable length of rope could not be found in the marina.

Luckily Vernon knew a local firefighter and one was produced, albeit at the last minute. Following the recent rain, it would prove to be a slippery spectacle.

Social activities like this was one of the few times when people from all three sectors of the marina came together, rather than an occasional wave or nod of acknowledgement as they walked or drove by. There was no hostility, they just led different lives, some preferred a quiet meditative existence, others the company of their small intimate group of friends. Many inhabited lives miles away from the marina, visiting their boats only at weekends and holidays, though, whether boaters or dwellers, they all had one thing in common, a desire to be afloat, and lead a slower and simpler way of life, albeit for some a short period of time.

The afternoon started with a bang literally, when during the bands opening song a fuse blew in one of the amplifiers. Bert who had begrudgingly agreed to sell raffle tickets was heard to remark loudly. 'Thank Christ for that. Bloody din.' Unfortunately for him it was quickly repaired, and the band played on.

Linda had not approached Luke and Ryan to contribute anything towards the event as she was still unsure of their present relationship. There was no doubt that Luke's brief association with Haseeb at the hospital had hurt Ryan a great deal. But true love runs deeper than a shallow stream and after time Ryan forgave his little indiscretion. Luke still thought fondly about his friendship with Haseeb and wondered how he was getting on in Manchester and if he had found a new partner to share his life with. Neither his name, nor the episode was ever mentioned again between the two of them.

The weather remained dry and warm throughout the afternoon. A few rogue nimbostratus clouds crept across the blue sky but dispersed as quickly as they had arrived. Many people from within and outside the marina came, and by the evening all those involved in the fund-raising event agreed it had been successful. The amount of money raised had exceeded expectations. This had been further boosted by an anonymous donation of one hundred pounds, which had been left with a note in an envelope on Linda's desk in the office. The barbeque and subsequent revelries went on well into the early hours of the morning, with disco music replacing the band.

At any social event, be it a party, wedding, or even a funeral there are always those who happily sit at the margins, only stepping out into the light when the final dance is played, or last orders called. This is how it was with Luke and Ryan on that warm evening, their close embrace demonstrating a relationship on the mend. Six months later, to the delight of all who knew them they would announce their intention to get married. Rita would not be on the guest list. Bert had attempted to express his view on same sex marriage, but a disapproving stare from Mur dissuaded him from doing so.

Some never made it back to their boat that night. One who shall remain nameless was found lying asleep in a ditch outside the marina. Another semi naked and giggling in the middle of a cabbage field. A third attempting to reach his boat tripped over the mooring line, ending up headfirst in the water. Thankfully there were people on hand to pull him out.

Did Jeb have any doubts and regrets about leaving Crockenhill Marina after so many years of living there? He probably did in those dark hours before a watery cold light intrudes in through the windows. He was after all a man of contemplation and there was much to contemplate on. In the end though there was little choice, he had to follow the signs wherever they may take him.
Where the signposts end, the trail begins. Marty Robins.

Of course, Jeb would miss his daily conversational duals with Bert and Bruce, and whilst he was sure he would meet new people on his journey he doubted, for good or bad, if another Bert character existed anywhere. He was given an assortment of farewell gifts, drank far too much and rambled his way through a thank you speech.

When a grey dawn crept silently across the sleepy aqua village it contrasted greatly to the previous day's jollification. It was well past midday before boat doors were thrown open and people stumbled into the ranch building in need of some refreshment. Bert was happy as the coffee machine had been repaired and he would not have to drink instant anymore. Everyone else was pleased as they would not have to listen to him complaining.

Jeb, Bruce, and Bert would never again meet to chew the cud over a cup of coffee. The following day Jeb along with Hazel and Sid slipped the lines on their boats and headed out of the marina for a new life up country. A small crowd of well-wishers waved them off. It was after all, the end of an era. Little did they realise that storm clouds were gathering across the land and two weeks into their journey the Government would announce a total lockdown due to the Corona Virus stranding them for many weeks near Oxford.

Bert, ever the cynic, told everyone that Jeb would be back. Maybe he would, but until that day, the three wise men would become two.

Printed in Great Britain
by Amazon

59066299R00115